Gracie and Marge:

Kicking the Bucket Together

Brenda Drexler

Gracie and Marge:
Kicking The Bucket Together

Copyright © 2021 by Brenda Drexler

2nd Edition

ISBN: 978-1-7374657-2-0

Website: **www. BRENDADREXLERAUTHOR. COM**

Email: BDREXLERWRITER@GMAIL.COM

Contents

Gracle and Marge...................

two 18

three 25

four 30

six 40

seven 52

eight 60

nine.......................................65

ten 70

eleven....................................73

thirteen 95

fourteen 102

fifteen..................................107

sixteen 116

seventeen............................121

twenty one 170

twenty two.........................173

Gracie and Marge

Gracie Gepper looked to be near death's door. Thin tubes were connecting her to beeping boxes and bags of fluid. Lights were flickering from equipment near the head of her bed. Marge stood beside the bed, tears rolling down her cheeks. She felt a little sick looking at the best friend she'd ever had in her whole life. She couldn't stop the tears from rolling down her face and dripping off her chin and nose.

"I can't lose my Gracie. Just can't," she whispered to herself.

Gracie was so limp and still that it reminded Marge of the first time they ever met, just about one year ago, in this same hospital. Not because she was quiet the first time they met. Oh no. She was mad then as Marge recalled, mad as all-get-out.

Marge had been sitting on the side of a bed next to Gracie's in the emergency room of University Hospital. A neighbor brought her there on his way to work because she slipped on the ice outside the back door to her apartment house and busted her elbow. He left her at the ER entrance bleeding all over her new fur coat she had just purchased that week at the Salvation Army Store for fifteen bucks. Marge really liked the good deals she could get there.

Anyhow, there Marge sat, moaning over her throbbing elbow, when they rolled Gracie into the room. She was giving hell to the world. That's one of the things Marge found out that she liked about Gracie…at least most of the time…when she gives hell, most everyone gets it. In no time, she was threatening to de-tooth a cute little guy in green scrubs who was poking her arm with a needle.

"Come on now, Miss Gracie," he coaxed. "Just let me do my job."

"You stringy little snot, get away from me or I'll be chewin my next steak with your teeth," Gracie yelled as she tried to push him away.

Don't know how many of them it took, but she finally got that shot. Marge managed to watch the whole thing by moving the curtain aside a little and scooting to the bottom of her own bed.

Yeah, Marge liked Gracie from the get-go. She found that Gracie could be a bit cantankerous, but likeable, in spite of herself.

Marge looked her over real good. She shook her head at the sight of the ugly gown that fits nobody, but everybody gets when they are admitted to the hospital. She thought that Gracie had an interesting face, which was toothless, round and wrinkled, especially her forehead. Out of that pruny little face came large, high cheekbones and a sticking-out kind of chin that meant business. Her hair was the color of second-day snow plastered to her head creating an unsightly scull-cap. Someone like Marge just had to feel sympathetic toward someone like Gracie.

Suddenly, those sharp blue eyes looked right into Marge's face, and her wrinkled lips flapped out at her.

"Who are you?" Gracie asked, in what Marge considered a commanding voice. She scared her to her feet.

"Hi, I'm Marguerite." She smiled at her, real big, and took a few cautious steps forward. Marge didn't know if her ER neighbor wasn't very-well ready to take out her teeth, too.

"Marguerite? What kind of name is that? What'd your mama call you, girl?"

"Well, you could call me Marge. Some people call me that."

She took a few more cautious steps toward Gracie's bed, not wanting to be overly familiar with a grouchy stranger, who sure wasn't in the best mood.

"Marge, I want ya ta look for my stuff, if'in ya don't mind."

"Look for what, Miss Gracie?" Marge asked, remembering the nurse calling her Miss Gracie.

"Listen, here, Marge. Look under my bed. They said they put my stuff under the bed, but I think they lied. Ya just can't trust people these days. They's liable to take my things for themselves or sell the whole kit'n caboodle. Look under there." Her finger pointed to under her bed.

Marge bent down slowly, looking for signs of Gracie's belongings. She bent way over, and, feeling a little dizzy, decided to squat for a closer look. With hands on both knees, and minding her sore elbow, she squatted until her bony butt almost touched the floor. She peered into the space below the bed but all she saw besides the underside of the bed was a bag of Gracie's pee hanging from the other side.

Marge didn't know what to make of that. She rose real slow, partly because she thought Gracie might be madder that hot coals since her stuff wasn't under the bed, and partly because she isn't all that young these days. When her eyes were level with the top-side of the mattress, she saw that Gracie was giving what-for to an enormous black woman in green scrubs who looked hefty enough to stuff Gracie's mouth into a matchbox. She started to squat back down until all the noise stopped but Gracie caught sight of the top of her gray head going down.

"Hey! Who is that? What ya doin down there?" she demanded.

Marge came up slowly, smiling a nervous smile. "It's me, Gracie. How ya feelin?"

"I ain't. I done gone and froze my dadgum hands and feet. What do ya think of that?"

She was staring straight into Marge's face. Waiting for some kind of response. Her toothless mouth clamped tight. Marge wanted to laugh because she thought Gracie's bottom lip stuck out like a little window ledge. But she didn't laugh. Gracie still seemed to be waiting for an answer.

"Well, gee, does it hurt?" Asked Marge. It was all she could think of saying, at the time.

"Of course it hurts, you dimwit. What do ya think? I'm suin. Don't think I'm not. Either that or I'm marchin down to that bus station and crackin that durned fool over the head with my violin. Who does he think he is, anyways? I ride a bus most of my life, and one day I don't have the fare, and I get bounced off like a criminal!"

Marge listened to the tirade of a woman she didn't know anything about, but already felt sorry for. Gracie's voice was sort of low but sounded strong. Then, Marge remembered about her things and felt bad that she hadn't found them for her.

"I'm really sorry, but your stuff ain't under the bed. I don't know where it is."

"My stuff? Why would my belongins be under the bed? Those arrogant sonsbcctchcs took my clothes right off my body, stripped me near naked, and threw all my things in a plastic bag. Who do they think they are, anyhow?"

She motioned for Marge to come closer, bending her crooked finger back and forth, and whispered something that Marge couldn't hear. Her blue eyes glared toward Marge's brown eyes. Marge was worried she was getting somewhat agitated, and hoped it wasn't with her. Gracie reached up and grabbed a handful of hair and gently pulled Marge closer to her face, and whispered.

"Check if ya see that bag out there in the hall, will ya? I think it was white, or maybe black."

Marge was usually compliant when people asked her to help, just her nature, and she thought that Miss Gracie might need a lot of help in her condition. So she crept around the corner to the hall and did, indeed, see a large black plastic bag. She supposed it was Gracie's, and walked towards it, but backwards, so as not to be noticed just in case anyone was watching out for the bag. She wrapped both hands around the top of the bag, completely forgetting her sore elbow, and walked back towards Gracie's bed, dragging a large, black garbage bag behind her.

"What do ya mean? This ain't my clothes. This is garbage. You think my stuff is garbage? I thought you looked like someone with more sense than that. Do I have ta get out of this bed and get my belongings, myself?"

Marge looked wide-eyed into the bag that was gaping open for her to look inside.

"Look here." Gracie pointed inside the bag. "Does this look like my stuff?"

"No Gracie, I'm sure it don't." Never actually having seen her stuff, she didn't know what to say to Gracie. "Maybe we should look, just in case."

They both peered into the dark bag, and Gracie perked up.

"Well," she said as she pulled out a red hairbrush. "Now ain't that a sassy-looking brush."

"Hey, that's nice. Let me look."

And Marge put her face even closer to the bag. "Honest to goodness, there's some nice things in this old bag. Lookie here, at this nice little powder compact and a mirror ... not exactly my color, but it'll do."

They were both fishing around in there for more treasure when a nurse came in and wrinkled her nose at the site of the bag on Gracie's bed. "Oh no. This just won't do," said the lady in white.

That bag was gone lickety-split, and Gracie was, too, soon after. Marge waved goodbye as Gracie was wheeled out, yelling all the way down to the elevator, "Where's my stuff. Give me my britches, for crying out loud. I didn't say nothing about wanting to stay here, anyways."

Marge decided to go home since her elbow didn't hurt anymore and, "Probably ain't broken any-o-how," she said to no one in particular. She wiped the dried blood off her arm, then slipped out of the Emergency Room without anybody paying any attention to her, at all.

But Marge had taken a liking to Miss Gracie. She was a strange bird, for sure. Marge didn't want to leave her alone there. Hard telling what would happen to her. Besides, it was snowing again, and she didn't want to go outside right that minute. Without really thinking about it, Marge hurried into the next elevator and pushed all the buttons. As the doors opened on each floor, she poked her head out and listened. Finally, the doors slid open on the fourth floor and she could hear Gracie's voice echoing down the hall.

"Where's my stuff, daggum? Who has my violin? Don't nobody want me mad if ya mess with my violin, folks? Uh, uh," she yelled.

Marge found a restroom around the corner from the elevators, and out of sight from the nurse's station, waiting till they had time to get Gracie settled into her room. She rested on the one seat available. Sitting there like that, though, reminded her of how it had been an awful long time, so, being the practical kind of person she is, Marge availed herself of the facilities and killed some time to boot.

When the coast was clear she moved quietly down the hall, peeping into rooms as she went, looking for Gracie's gray head. First gray head she spotted wasn't the right one. It belonged to a long, skinny woman who was sitting up in bed with her hands folded around a small milk carton in her lap. She was straight up but her eyes were closed. Marge touched the carton; it was warm. The skinny woman didn't look at her or move at all. She looked so pretty and peaceful Marge didn't want to disturb her. So, she backed out quietly so as not to be a bother. Marge thought for a second about getting a nurse for the lady, but decided to leave her be. Best thing, probably.

She looked in another room with no luck. The next room had one empty bed, and another bed with the curtain pulled partway. The person in that bed seemed to be in terrible pain. Marge had never heard such moaning and groaning as was coming from behind that curtain. She grabbed the side of the green curtain with her fingertips and stuck her chin over its edge just in time to look face to face with a very large, red-faced woman who appeared to be struggling with something underneath her.

"Howdy," said Marge.

"I'm glad you're here! I've been on this thing forever, and ain't nothin happened. You're just going to have to give me an enema like I told you to start," she demanded as she struggled to pull the bedpan out from beneath an enormous rear end. It looked to be stuck.

Well, Marge thought that one over for about a second and decided it wouldn't be a very good idea to try to help. They could both be hurt real bad, is what Marge figured.

"Someone will be here shortly, Hon, I'm sure," Marge said, as she remembered the warm milk carton, and backed out of the room.

It's a good thing Gracie was in the next room because Marge's nerves couldn't keep this up all night. Gracie looked to be sleeping, but her eyes popped open soon as Marge got to the side of her bed, causing Marge to jump back a foot.

"What are ya doin here?" She tried to sound gruff, but she was dopey.

"Just wanted to tell you goodbye before I left. Didn't get a chance to, downstairs. Did they give you a shot to make you sleepy?"

Gracie's eyes were at half-mast and she didn't answer. She was in a small room by herself. Marge looked around. Looking first in the bath room. "White," she announced to no one.

She opened the closet door. There were a mess of bags in there; a paper shopping bag from Lazarus, a plastic one with holes in it, a canvass bag stenciled, greyhound, and what looked like a violin case.

"Do you play the violin, Gracie?" Marge shouted across the room.

"Hm?" Her eyes opened just a little. "Of course, I do," she said softly.

Her voice sounded kind of drowsy-like. She wasn't as spunky as she was in the emergency room.

"Drugged," said Marge. "I'll come back again real soon, Gracie. Okay? I'll come see ya tomorrow."

She raised her left hand about an inch off the bed and dropped it.

Marge is sometimes forgetful, especially when she gets busy. Seems to be more forgetful as time goes by. So, she forgot about her promise to visit Gracie the next day, which was Sunday, but remembered her again on Monday. And that's when she went back to the hospital to see if Gracie was still there. Of course, Marge tried calling first, but they wouldn't tell her anything. She thought that was really unfair.

"Why can't you just tell me if Gracie is still there? How many Gracie's do you have there that have frostbite, for Pete's sake? Just because I don't know her last name? Like it's some big secret, or somethin." Marge paused to change her attitude a little, hoping for some sympathy.

"I'm sorry, but I don't have a lot of money and I'd have ta ride in the cold all the way downtown just to find out if she is or if she isn't in your hospital. I'm afraid to get frostbite my own self, don't ya know." Didn't help. So, she had to go there if she wanted to know anything more about that Gracie.

What made her remember about Gracie was that, when she walked down to the drugstore at Fourth and Central to buy some Marlboros, she thought to herself that she was going to freeze her nose right off her face, and that reminded her of Gracie who just about froze her feet and hands with frostbite. So, she went to the hospital, just about freezing everything while waiting on the Fourth Street bus.

Gracie was sitting up in her bed, griping at a chicken leg, when Marge walked into her room. "Hmmm, that sure does looks good," Marge said as she checked out the dinner tray.

"Then eat it!"

Without warning of any kind, Gracie flung that chicken leg right at Marge, who just barely grabbed it before it hit her in the face. She was right, too. It was good. So were the greens.

They were both playing around like silly little girls, licking their fingers, laughing at the sucking sounds they were making as they pulled their fingers out from between tight lips.

In between fingers, Gracie said, "Guess I gotta find me a new place. Can't go back to where I was. Gave everybody there what-for and don't think I'm welcome back."

"That's terrible, Gracie. Are you sure you can't go home?"

"Nope. Gotta find myself a new place to live. Guess I oughta try to stay in this darn hospital as long as I can. Spring would be a good time to get out. Whatcha think, Marge?"

Marge had an idea. She got so excited, all of a sudden, that she jumped off the bed causing all Gracie's tubes to jiggle and swing back and forth. Even her pee bag sloshed.

"Oh, Gracie! Oh, Gracie! I got a place! I got a place!"

She bobbed around the bed. She could barely control herself. She remembered something that she thought was wonderful. Gracie didn't need to be homeless. Marge knew where she could find a home. When she bobbed back to the side of the bed, Gracie reached out and grabbed her arm. Her grip made Marge believe she was strong enough to go home.

"What's the matter with ya, girl? That bouncin around is givin me the vertigo."

"I got a place for you, an apartment. Really it's a room, but it's big. And you'd have to share a bathroom with some other people in the apartment downstairs, but they're okay. It's a big house on Central Avenue, right across from the race track. Talk about a dream house. The family on the first floor has three blonde-headed kids, good kids. Big bathroom that you would share. And I'm upstairs, and we could play cards every night. Oh, this is the best thing that could possibly happen. Don'tcha think?"

Gracie's forehead wrinkled and her mouth screwed up like she was getting ready to whistle. She looked to be thinking seriously about this offer. Then she nodded her head and seemed to have come to a decision.

"Tell me more about these people who would be usin my bathroom. I'm a bit picky about who sits on my commode, ya know. I sleep till I feel like gettin up, and I don't like to be bothered with no noisy rug-rats or animals, if they got'em."

"Those little people are the best kids you'll ever meet. I promise. The little girl, she comes up and talks with me sometimes, like a little adult. Honest truth."

"Well, If ya play euchre, I'll give it a try."

Marge took a city bus to the hospital on Gracie's discharge day. She almost didn't recognize her new friend in regular clothes. But, there she sat in a chair, dressed and ready to go. She was wearing a heavy black coat and had her bags on the floor, at her side. What really got Marge's attention was the purple hat with ruffled edges on Gracie's head. And, Gracie had teeth.

"Gracie, ya look great! I'm lovin this hat. Ya look like a movie star or somethin."

"More like somethin, I suspect," grumbled Gracie.

The nurse, who Marge remembered from her last visit to see Gracie, was fussing around about some papers. Gracie finally said, "Just show me where to sign, will ya. My ride is here, and I'm ready ta go home."

The girls had already agreed to take a cab home, since Gracie had too much to lug around on a bus. "I'll be out front waitin for ya." A nurse, or whoever, wheeled Gracie to the ER entrance. The door and trunk of the cab were both open, waiting for passengers and belongings. When the trunk was loaded and they sat in the back seat of the cab, they looked at each other and smiled.

"You'll like your room. I just know ya will."

"I suppose I will. And I owe ya a big thanks for takin care of it all for me. That landlady of yours knows I'm comin today, don't she?

"Sure enough." Marge smiled.

"You're a good egg, Marge."

And they headed home.

two

And that was that. They became best friends. The girls played a bunch of euchre, took lots of walks around the neighborhood, watched movies, and did just about everything together. And Gracie took a shining to those little kids downstairs. Of course, they each had stuff they did separately – they weren't Siamese twins. Marge would go to Churchill Downs nearly every day when the races were on. She knew how to get in free. Sometimes, she'd get lucky and somebody leaving would hand her a racing program. One time, a fella handed her a pass to a box seat. Marge acted like that sort of thing happened every day of the week.

"Some days are just full of blessins," she said, as she thanked the fella.

And, Gracie, she liked to wander around downtown a lot of days. Marge would be at the paddock talking to the horses. Gracie would be walking or riding the bus around downtown or playing her music where-ever she rested.

That's the only time Marge ever knew of her playing that violin in those days. She played pretty, too. Sometimes Marge would go with her. She'd plumb wear Marge out. About the only time she stopped moving was when she parked herself and her bags on a bench to play some music. Yeah, some people would stop to listen and clap their hands when she was done. Others would scurry by as if they were embarrassed. She didn't seem to ever notice them. But, she sure saw the money some of them left in her violin case.

Sometimes, Gracie would go with Marge to the races, but she didn't care much for the horses. Marge thought that was a shame, since Gracie was missing out on knowing how wonderful horses were. She did talk about going to the dog races in Florida once, long ago, with a fella she was sweet on.

"Yep, that's what made me buy a bag with that skinny old greyhound on it," she'd said. "Was thinkin about that good-lookin, good-for-nothin, one day, as I passed through the bus station. There was a young lady sellin these bags. I don't know if her sellin the bags was on the up-and-up, but it felt like a premonition or somethin, so I just went on and bought it. My goodness, he would be an old man by now."

They had themselves some good times since they became friends. They'd always be on the lookout for fun stuff to do. "No time like the present to live a good life," they would say. Two peas in a pod, practically. You should hear them when they both would laugh themselves silly every time one of them brings up the night they crouched behind a dumpster for a heck of a long time, scared to death, waiting for the cops and everyone else to clear out. Neither of them was in any mood to go to jail, but a busing protest seemed like a good way to spend a Friday night.

"They say it'll be a mess of people there," Gracie said, all excited-like. "Bonfires and everthin. And I got a few things to say about these buses, don't think I don't. That one darned driver put me right off that bus and caused me to land in the hospital. Won't never be forgetting that."

Of course, Marge reminded her that was how they met. "So it must been fate or something." Gracie would just shake her head. She would do that anytime Marge talked about fate. Gracie isn't one to talk about the power of fate, not a believer.

So, off they went to their first big, and hopefully last, protest.

"Don't this feel sorta awkward, ridin a bus to a busing protest, and all," Marge asked Gracie.

"Just keep your eyes on that driver. He's got no complaint about us goin to a protest. Shoot. He might show up there, hisself." Gracie and Marge both covered their mouths with their hands to muffle a laugh. Gracie knows she can be humorous sometimes.

So they rode the bus to get to the high school where all the doings was to be. They sat in the back and didn't talk much. Kept their eyes on the driver, though. Neither of them were sure what went on at these affairs. They were just winging it.

"If there's gonna be a bonfire," said Marge, "then I'm sure there's gonna be hotdogs roastin. Too bad I didn't have a single hotdog in my fridge. I brought these marshmallows. I figured I might make a trade." She pulled out the half-filled bag of marshmallows for Gracie to see. But, the truth is, that whole protest was not a thing like either of them expected.

"These people's crazy," Gracie screamed in Marge's ear. "Why in the world would they want the buses to stop runnin? I need the buses to get around, and ain't nobody forcin me to get on one. Don't make no sense. Ain't no way to solve nothin."

The two of them couldn't make head nor tails out of anything going on there. Signs, t-shirts, and people all shouting about no more busing. They were both wondering how poor old Gracie would get downtown without the buses? So they went looking for the bonfires, hoping to find food roasting and happier people, when another kind of yelling started up.

Marge was more than a little scared. "It's just like in the movies, but a whole lot scarier."

 The police were jumping out of the backs of vans. People were scattering in all kinds of directions. They jumped out with guns in their hands, big guns. Marge grabbed Gracie's arm, and started pushing through the crowd.

Now, they've both been in some predicaments in their time, but this was something else, again. They just wanted to get out of there and go home, but were being pushed ever which way. The both of them were being turned so many times they were getting dizzy. Some of the others in the crowd were just as scared, and some were mad and seemed ready to fight.

It didn't take long for Marge and Gracie to be done with this whole protest. "Me, I say the bus company can take care of itself without us gettin killed over it," yelled Gracie.

They saw two young women scoot behind a large, green dumpster and figured there was room for two old women, too, so Gracie and Marge managed to break through the crowd. The four of them squatted there for a real long time, not making any noise. Except for Gracie. She had a sensitive nose.

"Gawd! It stinks back here," she complained.

"Shh," cautioned one of the girls behind the dumpster with them.

Gracie shook her head and wrinkled her nose. "It is mighty smelly back here." agreed Marge. Someone pass gas?"

Their dumpster partners, both in their thirties, seemed real serious and real scared. They both wore T-shirts. One shirt said, HONK FOR HONKIE and the other said, STOP FORCED BUSING. They listened to yelling and feet running right past their little hiding place. And, they all held their breath with eyes wide open when some people stopped near the dumpster. The two young women left when they heard voices they recognized. They asked if Gracie and Marge wanted to go with them, but they'd both had enough of their protest business, even if they were real nice. They hunkered down a bit longer, till they felt like it was all over, when all the shouting stopped.

"The buses better not stop runnin fore we get outta here," worried Gracie.

"Dad-gum, that garbage stinks to high heaven. Whatcha think's in there?" It just made me think of my stomach and those hotdogs I didn't get.

"Want some marshmallows?"

Marge pulled the flattened bag out of her coat pocket, and they ate. Good thing about marshmallows, being smashed never hurt their taste. Marge was rolling one around in her mouth.

"I wonder why they're called marshmallows. Why not mush puffs or snow somethin?" Gracie didn't answer. By the time the mush puffs were gone, they were ready to go.

They stood for the first time in about thirty or more minutes, both using the red-brick wall and the dumpster for support as they worked at straightening up their bodies. It was quiet enough there that they could hear each other's bone popping, which made them snicker a bit, in between moans and groans.

They turned the corner and walked right into a cop. Big guy. Looked a bit like Kojak.

"You ladies lost?"

They stopped in their tracks and held their breath. Turned out he was very nice to them and they relaxed a little. He drove them up to Dixie Highway, just in time to catch a bus home. They didn't mention the protest to him or the bus driver. Learned their lesson.

"I'll never get messed up in anythin like that again, that ain't none of our business," said Gracie. "Ain't got no dog in that race. Just glad to be alive."

"He was just the cutest policeman I've ever seen, and so nice." Marge was already over the protest.

<u>three</u>

Gracie and Marge made a habit of enjoying themselves, had some good times. Marge looked at Gracie lying in the hospital bed and hoped it wasn't all about to end now. "Gettin old is hell," she thought. She was worried about Gracie, who looked real sick, her face was pale, and her body so still on the bed like that, quiet and all. She'd heard of hypothermia but never knew anyone that got it. Marge had left her alone for a few days to visit her sister, Valleen, in Bowling Green. She had tried to get Gracie to go, but she said there wasn't a thing there she needed to see. That Gracie, she's like that a lot.

"If she said it once, she'd said it a hundred times, that if she'd done been someplace, and it wasn't good enough for her to stay, then there was no reason to go back. I just like to go anywhere, when I can," Marge said to no one in particular.

Marge's sister had tried to get her to move to Florida with her. Marge came back to see what Gracie thought of the idea. At this point, they were so close that Marge couldn't even imagine moving without Gracie. No way.

She pulled an old wooden chair close to Gracie's bed and watched her for a long time. Gracie didn't move. Marge examined the tubes and bags hanging from a metal pole. She checked for the pee-bag, and sure enough found it. Always gotta be one. She was getting antsy.

"Gracie. Can you hear me?" She still didn't move. "Gracie, would you like to go to Florida with me and Valleen? There's no hypothermia in Florida. It's real warm there."

Marge turned away from the hospital bed to find a tissue. Both her nose and eyes were draining at the same time, and her throat hurt, a big knot made it hard to swallow. She blew her nose a couple of times, and when she turned back around, Gracie's eyes were open just a little bit.

"Oh, God, Gracie. I thought you was a goner. What're you doin scarin me like that?"

"If ya listen to them, I pert near was a goner," she whispered. "Don't matter no way. What am I gonna do, Marguerite? They're gonna put me away. I'm a ward now," she whispered with such sadness that Marge had to fight back her tears.

"What do ya mean, put away? And what is this ward stuff? You got a nice little room here."

"Ask 'em, out there!"

She pointed to the hall and closed her eyes. A tiny little drop of salty water ran down the side of her face and disappeared into her thin gray hair. Marge dabbed the tear with her tissue and watched her awhile, and when Gracie slept, Marge went out into the hall.

"What's wrong with Gracie Gepper?" she asked.

The youngish nurse looked up from her stack of papers and smiled like she didn't mean it. "Oh, she's going to be okay, dear. No need to worry."

"Then why," she demanded, "is she goin to be put out in a ward? She is terrible worried about that."

The starchy nurse wrinkled her forehead and appeared to be thinking real hard about something while looking over Marge's shoulder. Marge turned quickly to see if she was looking at something back there. Her wrinkles disappeared and her smile was back. "Oh, I see what you mean, now. Are you a relative?"

Not missing a beat, Marge was way ahead of this question.

"I am her only livin relative, her cousin."

"Well, let's see if Ms. Gepper will give me permission to talk to you."

That nurse got so professional, now, making Gracie sign a paper so she could talk in front of Marge. Poor Gracie, could barely hold the pen. Marge was really hoping she wouldn't tell the nurse she didn't have any cousins. Marge does hate telling a lie, and really hates getting caught at it.

Turns out, Gracie had been made a ward of the state because people at the hospital and the state people thought she couldn't take care of herself anymore. Just because she keeps ending up in the emergency room. "Needs someone to watch over her," the nurse said.

"What does that mean, exactly?" Marge asked, even though she was afraid she already knew.

"She will be going to a nursing home from here so that she will be cared for properly."

Gracie turned away and said nothing.

"This wouldn't happen if she was twenty-five instead of old, would it? Don't you know, old people have feelins, too? Don't people know that?"

Marge felt the tears pouring from her eyes. "A discharge planner will be here, shortly, to talk with your both. Let me know if you need anything." She smiled a quick smile, then patted Gracie on the arm and returned to her station. Marge's heart hurt more than she thought she could bear. She didn't know what to do, so she kissed Gracie's hand and went home.

four

Marge cried all the way home. She thought about how Gracie would never ride around downtown on the bus again. "Oh, Gracie," she sobbed as she rocked back and forth, using her sleeve for tears and sniffles. "Poor, poor Gracie," she cried at her kitchen table. "I should never of left ya alone." She quietly eased down the stairs to Gracie's apartment, found her violin, put all her things into bags, took them upstairs and pushed them under her bed.

Except for Gracie's Social Security check. She knew it was still in the apartment, because they always walked together to the post office, where Gracie had a P.O. Box, and then go to the liquor store to cash it. Marge stashed that in a safe place and walked the two blocks down Central Avenue to the liquor store where they usually cashed their checks.

Marge moseyed around the store waiting for most people to leave before she walked to the counter. She picked up and put back chips and candy and other stuff, waiting for the place to clear out. But, before she could hand the man behind those metal bars the check that she had signed, she got real scared, stuffed the check back in its safe place and hurried home.

Everyone in the building heard the shudder of old wood hit old wood when the landlady, Ms. Harbo, closed the door to Gracie's first floor room. The key rattled in the lock before it snapped the bolt shut. She made so much racket, Marge could hear her all the way upstairs in her apartment. The stairs creaked and groaned as Ms. Harbo slowly climbed the foutrted worn steps. Marge waited in silence, standing on the other side of her door.

"Ms. Cater, you home?" as she pounded on the door, making the hinges rattle.

Landlady or not, she was a nosy old hag, and if Marge didn't open the door she would unlock it and sashay on in, and wouldn't be the least surprised if she saw her standing right there inside.

"What do you want, Ms. Harbo?" Marge demanded, as she blocked the doorway with her barely-big-enough-to-do-it body.

The landlady was breathing real hard through her mouth from the climb, noisily exhaling and inhaling.

"Just wondering if you knew where Ms. Gepper's belongings went to. Ain't nothin hardly at all in her room."

"What do ya want with Gracie's things, Ms. Harbo? Ya know she don't like nobody messin with her stuff."

"Someone called me, that's all. They're takin her to a home, you know. No family to call, unless you know of some kin? They said they thought there was a cousin, but can't find hide-nor-hair of her."

Marge thought about the little bit Gracie had shared about her family, little snippets here and there. She'd gone to a lot of schools; her mama was real sickly; her daddy taught her the violin. Marge knew she and Gracie were born in the same area of town, the West-end. But, as Gracie put it, she was born… a "few years earlier" than Marge.

"Sorry, don't know any cousins or nothin."

Ms. Harbo went on talking and Margewent on not paying her much notice. Mainly, Marge was hoping the landlady wasn't going to have a heart attack right in front of her. Marge had a lot on her mind. A lot to do.

"Well! Do you know if she cashed her check or not?" boomed Ms. Harbo.

"Oh, I'm pretty sure she cashed it, all right. But you know, I'm sure you know, I been outta town a while. And I think she was mugged or somethin, and lost most of her stuff. A person ain't safe even opening her own door these days. I think we need better locks on our doors here, too. You should see about that, Ms. Harbo, don'tcha think? And Gracie, she's pretty old, you know."

She ignored Marge's suggestion for new locks and grabbed the railing with both hands for the climb down. The stairs groaned under each foot-fall. Ms. Harbo was a slow-moving, heavy lady.

"Oh my," she complained. "Oh, mercy me."

Marge locked her door. She didn't leave the apartment for days. She was so afraid someone would find out about Gracie's check that she kept it stuffed in her bra the whole time. She laughed at the memory of when she forgot about a pair of earrings she had tucked in her bra one time. They were lost near a week. But she wouldn't forget the check, no way. Time passed and no one came after her, so she finally went out. She had a lot to do.She'd been thinking about this whole, terrible situation. She and Gracie are better than sisters, and can tolerate each other really well. She helps Gracie, and Gracie helps her. "Ain't no sense, at all, in her getting stuck in a crummy old nursin home. She'd hate that, real bad," thought Marge. So, she needed a plan.

She called her sister who had already gone to Florida without her. She said that she had to take care of her good friend. It came to her like a dream while she was holed up in her room. Marge was out of food except for a package of crackers and a half bottle of gin. She was finishing those off and looking all sad at Gracie's violin, which she had gotten out from under the bed because it was so pretty and all. Like a flash, it came to her. Not the actual details, mind you. They sort of popped up as she needed them.

It took her some time to work it all out in her head. She got Gracie's violin out every day so she wouldn't forget, as she's prone to do sometimes. She felt so good one of those times, she propped Gracie's instrument on her shoulder and played until she cried from joy. Didn't sound anything like when Gracie Gepper played, but it sure made Marge cry.

five

"Excuse me. I'd like to see Ms. Gracie Gepper."

The nurse turned to look and Marge knew she was impressed. Marge was dressed in her best clothes. She had on red lipstick which she thought had always looked good on her ever since she was a young thing. And even though it was somewhat warm out, she was wearing white gloves, pearl buttons, buttoned. She had on a white sweater with pop-bead pearls around her neck, and a blue skirt. She doesn't wear skirts much these days, but this was a special occasion. The only problem was her shoes. All she had nice was a pair of white sneakers she got last month at the Dollar General, but she figured the top of her looked so good, no one would get around to looking at the bottom of her.

"Excuse me?" the nurse said, repeating what Marge had just said.

Marge always wondered why people did that. Could go on forever if you're not on to it.

"I'd like to visit with Ms. Gepper. I'm her cousin, from out of town. And I'd like to visit with her outside, if it's all right with you, ma'am. I have a condition and can't stay inside closed places too long, you see."

She fanned her face with one of her white gloves to stress the point.

The nurse smiled. Nice. "She's in room 119. It's up to her if she wants to go out, but it would be good for her. And it is such a nice day. The patio is to the left of this station." She pointed to a glass sliding door not too far away.

When Marge saw her, she made the Sign of the Cross. Gracie used to do that a lot and it seemed like the thing to do. Gracie was dressed in a gray sweat-suit, and Marge noted how glad she was about that. Marge had pictured that she would be in one of those gawd-awful gowns, and that could be a problem. Could be a little iffy getting out of there and through the bus station with her hind-in hanging out for the whole world to see. Especially if they had to make a run for it.

"Hello, Gracie, I'm your cousin from out of town, and I want to visit with ya for a while," she said loud enough for the nurse to hear.

The familiar old pruny face squinched up at Marge, and she laughed. She couldn't help it. Marge finally laughed at Gracie's bottom lip. She always was afraid someone might leave money on her lip instead of in the violin case after she played her music. Marge was so nervous from what she was doing that she couldn't help but laugh. You know how sometimes people just start laughing and giggling at funerals because they're so uptight? That was Marge.

"What the heck you laughin at? And, I ain't got no cousin. What's wrong with ya, girl?" She ended by blowing air through fish-lips.

"Shhh," Marge whispered close to her ear. "We're goin outside, Gracie. We really need to go outside."

"I don't need to go outside!" she yelled as she flung her arms around. "I've seen their outside. It ain't no bigger than a bathtub. A waste of time. No place to go. Nothin to see. Go look for yourself."

"OK, ya ain't my cousin, you're the best friend I've ever had. You've got to go out with me. And don't make no more noise. I brought your things, your violin. I want ya to play for me, but not in here."

"Ya got my things?"

Her hands quivered as she grabbed hold of Marge's. "I thought these sonsbeetches done kept my things for themselves. There's no respect here, Marge. No respect for nothin. Can't play my music in here. Not enough air in here for music," she spat out and shook her head side to side.

She shuffled her way over to the wheelchair Marge had brought in from the hallway. At first Marge thought she was going to have to ask for help. She sure didn't want to do that. No attention, is good attention. She rolled the chair and Gracie back and forth, up and down the hall, pretending to talk about the weather, until the nurse disappeared into a room down the hallway.

"Here we go," Marge whispered to the gray head in front of her. "I got you a surprise when we get out of here to safety. You're going to love it."

The two of them picked up speed as they passed the patio doors, which slid open and hung there, waiting. At the end of the hall were double doors, and on the other side of them, waiting for its passengers, was a cab with its back door wide open. Gracie gripped the arms of the chair and leaned forward. Marge was breathing hard and sweating in her gloves.

About a yard from the doors, a tall, thin man, coming from the lobby, stepped out in front of them, just about causing a dreadful crash.

"I'm so sorry," he said several times.

Gracie never took her eyes off the doors, kept leaning forward, saying nothing.

"Here, allow me," the tall man offered.

His long, bony hands gripped the bar on the door. Marge stared at his hands until he pushed the door wide open. Then she pushed the chair as fast as she could toward the cab. Gracie took so much time getting into the cab, with some groaning and some "Umphs" that Marge figured they might need that chair later. She folded it and threw it in to the front seat.

Everything they both owned was in the trunk of the cab. Their tickets out of town, to a warmer, kinder place, were in Marge's purse.

"We're going to Florida, Gracie. No hypothermia in Florida. I got an address right here for the Breezy Palms Mobile Home Resort Park, where Valleen lives. We'll get us a place there, too. How ya doin, Gracie? Ya okay?"

Her head was bobbing up and down slowly. She stroked her violin case. And then, Gracie reached over and patted Marge's hand, causing tears to roll out of her eyes and a knot to fill her throat.

"You are my best friend ever, too, Marge. For sure."

Marge looked into the eyes in the rear-view mirror.

"Greyhound Bus station." She waved a Ten Dollar bill. Fast as ya can!"

six

At first, Marge was really glad to get out of the cab and in to the bus station, another step closer to Florida. She thought about how Valleen would be so excited to see them, and that they'd finally be safe from…well, whoever might be out looking for them right about now. That's what she tried not to let Gracie in on. She was scared out of her skin but didn't want Gracie to know it. She wanted Gracie to think she had everything under control. And so far, things were going pretty well for them.

They had been in a rush to get to the bus station, and now they were sitting and waiting. Marge wanted to get out of town and out of reach of whoever might want to catch up with them. She definitely didn't want to go to jail for kidnapping Gracie from that nursing home.

So they took turns looking out for their belongings while the other got to walk around. Gracie came back from her break snickering and shaking her head.

"Mercy me," she said, covering her mouth with one hand and wiping her eyes with the other. "Durned fool. I can't even believe it."

"Believe what, Gracie?" Having no idea what had happened since she was on guard duty for the last hour. It would be hard to say what Gracie might have been up to.

"Mercy!" she said again. "Lookie over there. See, by the pop machine. See that shiftless ole coot; he was flirtin with me, the dimwit."

She continued to shake her head, but looked like she was having fun with the whole thing. She also realized that it felt pretty darn good to have anyone flirt with her.

"So, did ya hit him over the head with your purse; what'd ya do?" Marge was anxious for a good story. She looked in the direction Gracie had indicated. She was already imagining what it all looked like, with Gracie bopping the guy over the head with her heavy purse.

"Naw, I didn't hit the ole coot, just told him to get on with his smelly old self. Feel sorta shameful 'bout that, though. It did make me laugh a little. It's sure been a good long time since someone tried to get it on with Gracie Gepper."

"Well, I would'a thought you'd sock him or somethin." Marge was a little disappointed not to hear a good story. "Oh well, why don't we move our stuff over to that little café over yonder and get us some food. I'm feeling mighty shaky, and I can't take this waitin in one spot. I want to be on that bus so bad."

Gracie was hungry, too, happily slurping down her beef stew and sopping the juice up with her bread. Marge looked up when she noticed Gracie stopped eating to stare at a kid across from them, at another table. A teenager. A runaway, probably. Gracie looked at Marge, raised her eyebrows and tilted her head toward the kid, like Marge could read eyebrow sign language.

"What?" asked Marge.

"Ya think she's hungry? Think she's a runaway like us?"

Marge sucked in air. She didn't know Gracie knew they were running, maybe, from the law or somebody. Marge stared at Gracie, and felt sweat bead up on her forehead.

"How do I know? Don't know nothin about her. Just don't look."

Marge looked up, her eyes wide as saucers surprised by her friend's risky actions. Gracie nodded her head at the girl and spoke. Marge felt her stomach roll and almost threw up her soup.

"Hey, girlie. Ya hungry?" asked Gracie.

The kid looked down at an empty cup on the table in front of her. Gracie didn't let up.

"Ya by yourself?" she wasn't ready to let it go so easy.

The kid looked up, half smiled and said," Thanks, I'm ok."

"Just sayin, we're about to order some dessert. Want to sit with us and share? There'll be plenty."

Marge broke out in a terrible sweat, from head to toe, and was looking back and forth tween the kid and Gracie. "No good comin of this," she whispered to Gracie.

The kid stood up and moved toward their table. "Hi, I'm Josie."

"My goodness," Marge said in a long, drawn out Southern drawl. Her eyes were wide, staring down the kid. Marge's mouth was on autopilot with that one.

The child had legs like a giraffe. Marge was wondering where she got jeans to cover them. She was cute as a button, a long button, that is. Shiny brown hair, hanging well below her shoulders. "Like a dark waterfall," thought Marge, to herself. Large, beautiful brown eyes, like a doe looking into its mother's eyes.

By the time the three of them shared half a pecan pie, they knew the kid was running from home, had a mean step-dad and a mom who was scared of him, got beat up a bit today by her no-good step-dad, and was afraid of going to a foster home if anyone found out. Gracie just shook her head slowly side to side when the kid mentioned the foster home. She'd been there and done that.

"There's good foster homes and not-so-good, and some real damn bad. Pretty risky to get yourself into 'the system,'" said Gracie. Marge noticed the sad look on

Gracie's face, and felt the sadness for her friend. She knew Gracie had been in foster homes as a child.

After a few adjustments to their plans the three of them got all comfy on the bus. Marge looked around at the cushioned seats and other niceties. She poked Gracie on the elbow.

"Lookie, it's even got a toilet in the rear…sort of funny, huh, a toilet in the rear." Gracie didn't laugh at Marge's poke, so Marge just went on observing the bus and its inhabitants.

Marge noticed that Josie was reading the funnies from the newspaper that Marge had picked up from the counter in the little café, and was hoping Josie wouldn't bother her word scramble puzzle.

Gracie was real firm about this kid going to Florida with the two of them. Marge was pondering that and assumed that it was probably some of those issues that Gracie was carrying around, reminding her of herself. "Who knows," thought Marge. "I hear a lot, in the movies and TV, about us all havin issues. I just like livin day to day; more enjoyable that way."

Gracie said Josie could make up her own mind down there, where she was safe and warm, whether she wanted to stay or go back home to her good-for-nothing family. Truth is, neither of them knew what they were going to do with her when they landed in Florida. Valleen didn't have that much room and was already looking for a place for them. "Oh well," thought Marge.

Josie became their niece so people wouldn't be asking her, or Marge and Gracie, a bunch of questions.

"I've lied in my time, but not so many times in one day; and this has already been one long day, for sure," Marge leaned closer to Gracie and whispered. "The kid seems ok travelin with us, just makes me a bit uneasy travelin with a fugitive child. "

"It'll be alright Marge. You worry too much," said Gracie, without opening her eyes from her pretend nap.

Watching Josie read her paper made Marge wonder what she, herself, was doing at Josie's age? She was soon dreaming about jumping rope with a friend and then playing hopscotch when she darned near smacked her face on the seat in front of her when the bus brakes screeched to a halt at a bus stop with a little diner.

"Yuck. Can you smell the back of that dirty old seat?" But Gracie was up and heading to the exit door of the bus before Marge realized she was gone.

"Tell me more about Florida, Aunt Marge," Josie asked when they sat at the diner to eat. Josie had her chin propped on her hand looking like she was mighty interested. Marge told her what she knew about Florida and talked about Valleen while she and Gracie split a hamburger and Josie had a cup of tomato soup.

Marge was amazed at how the child had no problem play- acting with strangers. So she told her how the weather is nice most of the year. And how beautiful the ocean is. "You'll likely love Florida. Lot'sa people wear their swim suits most of the time, at least those livin near the beach." Marge couldn't think of anything else to tell Josie.

They were already in their seats when some new folks climbed onto the bus. A middle aged man in a suit, carrying a satchel, and a good-looking young fella in cowboy boots boarded. The man in the suit looked worried for another hundred miles or so. There were all types of people on the bus; families, old people, young people, some looking happy, some not. There was also a crying, tantrum-fitting little boy.

Now, it's not that Gracie and Marge don't like kids in general, well not all the time anyway, but they were probably not the only ones wanting to throw the kid from the bus, bless his heart. It was another stop before that munchkin was able to get his family off the bus. Mostly the bus was quiet, except for some light snoring and the occasional soft whimpering from the one infant on board.

Gracie sat in the seat with Josie after the diner, but that was okay with Marge. She wanted to take a nap anyway. She tried to imagine what Gracie already knew; what it feels like and what does it do to a kid to have to run away from family? Josie said she would miss her baby brother, but no one else. "Rotten bunch of people. Darned shame," thought Marge.

Marge asked Gracie if she had a plan for what they were going to do with a runaway teenager when they got to Florida. Marge thought of all sorts of negative possibilities.

"What about school? What if she needs to go to a hospital? What'll we do?"

"We got time to figure out somethin. Don't worry so much, Marge. You done pretty good so far. You're a darn good planner. You saved me, didn't ya?"

The next stop was uneventful. Restroom breaks, a little snack, stretching out from sitting so long on the bus. It was the getting back on the bus that was most interesting. They had noticed Josie talking to the young fella in cowboy boots over by the video games at the bus stop. She, laughing, smiling, and flipping her hair. He, thumbs in the pockets of his jeans, smiling big with white teeth, then smoothing her hair away from her eyes. Looked like a piece of trouble brewing for Aunts Marge and Gracie.

Gracie elbowed Marge, "Dang, I didn't count on this sort of shenanigans. She says she'll be eighteen in a couple a weeks. That might take care of a lot of our worries."

"I thought we wasn't supposed to be worried. Now I am, again."

By the time they made their way back to their seats, the cowboy now occupied the seat next to Josie.

"Lookie there," whispered Marge. "What do you think of that?"

"Aunt Gracie, Aunt Marge," whispered Josie from across the aisle. "This here is Cody. He just got out of the Army a few months ago and lives on a farm with his momma."

"Howdy, ma'am's," and he tipped his hand to his forehead just like he was wearing a cowboy hat, but he wasn't. He had slid it onto the shelf about the seats. "I was just telling Josie," he looked at her and smiled, "about our farm and my momma and little sisters and brother. My momma's a good woman; goes to church twice a week."

Marge was wondering why he was telling all this stuff about people they don't expect to ever meet. Gracie's bottom lip puffed up and her eyes were squinching and staring a hole right through that boy.

"Where's that farm you're talking about?" she asked.He didn't hesitate. "Well ma'am, I don't know how familiar you are with the great state of Georgia, but our place is just west of the town of Sparks. That would be north of Valdosta, and that is about 35 or 40 mile, or so, before you land in Florida."

He smiled some more. Josie smiled a lot. Marge was starting to feel like she was in a fog, thinking that maybe something important was happening, but couldn't get her mind wrapped around it just yet.

"Well, that's dandy," muttered Gracie, and closed her eyes.

"Did you hear that, Gracie? That girl was a cooin like a dove." Marge thought Gracie had a good idea and settled in for a nap, pulling her jacket up around her chin.

"Ouch! Whatcha doin?"

Marge jumped in her seat, awakened from a sound sleep by Josie wailing. "What? What's goin on?" asked Marge, still blinking her eyes.

Gracie had a hold of Josie's belly button, actually some kind of ring in her belly button that Marge had surely not noticed before that moment.

"Well, that's new," said Marge. "Matter of fact, I'd never seen Josie's belly before now, either. She either changed clothes or taken off some layers while I was sleepin."

Gracie's pointing finger still had a hold of Josie when she asked, "What's goin on tween you two, Josie? Ya don't know him long enough to trust anything he says."

"He's a good person, Aunt Gracie. I can feel it. There's a tenderness in his eyes."

Gracie let go of Josie's belly button. Josie rubbed her belly, checking out the piece of jewelry hanging there. Marge fixed her eyes on that thing, couldn't take them off that shiny bauble hanging from Josie's belly. She was trying to imagine how that'd hurt like the dickens to punch a hole in her belly. "My momma would'a killed me. These kids sure do a whole lot of things that hurt, just to decorate their bodies. My, my."

Josie squatted down by their seat.

"I like him a lot. He wants me to meet his momma and the rest of the family. The two of you have been so nice to me, never had anyone be so nice, and I really appreciate that. Now that I've met Cody, seems to me that there must be a lot more good people I need to meet."

Neither of them would have ever expected what happened next. That little girl, who was scared and alone just earlier that day, took Marge and Gracie's hands and kissed them both. Marge saw Gracie give Josie's hand a little squeeze and so she did the same. Josie went back to her seat, snuggled up against her cowboy with a smile on her face. While Marge was asleep, Josie the runaway, ran away, again.

"They got off the bus while ya was asleep and I pretended to be. At least she knows how ta leave if things aren't right," Gracie said. "He did seem to be a kind boy. And, I guess, that's that."

Marge thought Gracie's eyes looked a little wet and her own started stinging. They both prayed for her that night, and some nights after that, just that she'd be happy and peaceful, and remember two pretend aunts that really cared.

<u>seven</u>

And then a tire blew.

"Tarnation. What now?"

It was a loud bang, and they all held on tight to keep from being thrown from their seats. The bus driver was sliding and twisting all over, arms wrapped around that steering wheel. The bus went this way and that way and finally came to a stop, dust clouds covered the whole bus. They were in Florida, but not where they wanted to be.

They were a grumbling bunch at first. The girls were tired and achy all over. So they sat on their luggage and waited. They had been doing a lot of that, waiting. And speaking of waiting, seems that the twisting and turning caused a long line of passengers at the back of the bus. Marge was wishing she had one of those pee bags of her very own, right about then.

"Do you remember your pee-bag? Don't you wish you had one now?" asked Marge.

"Don't wanna remember any of that," said Gracie. "And yes I do."

"Do you think its fate, Gracie, that we met Josie, and that she met Cody, and this flat tire, and us waitin here in this ugly place?"

She stared down at the dusty ground, but wasted no time setting her friend straight on fate.

"Ain't no such thing as fate. Everyday happens, that's all. It is what it is, and that's that. We get up the next day just to see what it is and get on with it. You think too much, Marge."

Gracie got up and walked off stretching a little. Marge walked the other way, looking around and thinking that, maybe, it wasn't such an ugly place. Sort of interesting, maybe. Some scruffy - looking pine trees a ways off, and grass that didn't much look like grass. Not ugly, just different. And she supposed that maybe that ought to be okay.

Soft music began to fill the air. Marge stopped in her tracks, it was a few moments before she could make sense of it. She just stood there and listened, looking around, and suddenly, the place she thought was ugly became beautiful, almost. People on the bus looked out the windows, others sat or stood and listened in the shade of the bus, to Gracie's music making the day a little bit softer. Her face looked peaceful, her eyes closed softly. Seemed everybody on that bus knew how to smile. And don't you know, some put dollar bills in her violin case. Gracie can draw a crowd.

Later, while the tire was getting fixed by a guy in greasy overalls, and gnawing on chew tobacco, the two friends sat and rested in the shade. People who had watches studied them. Others ate anything they had stashed for the trip. Grating on Marge's slightly irritable side, Gracie had taken to using eyebrow language on this trip, and Marge just had to wait till it all played out to figure out what she was trying to say. So, Gracie raised her brows and nodded her head to a young couple that had packed real food for their trip.

And then Gracie started, "Oh, Marge, I'm so hungry my belly is hurtin bad. Don't we have nothin at all in the bag, dear?"

"We sure don't. We're just gonna have to wait till the next stop, I suppose. Do ya think you can make it, Gracie?" She moaned, and groaned. Marge thought she looked to be moving her body around like a snake; she never saw such a thing in her life, but was right proud of her for it. In just a few minutes they were enjoying a chicken salad sandwich and ice-tea, and someone else gave them some chocolate-chip cookies. Gracie was full very quickly and couldn't even finish the banana that the bus driver gave her. Good people everywhere. Apparently, for them, it wasn't such a bad place to stop, after all.

Between bites, Gracie asked about Valleen, "Tell me about that sister of yours. Is she tolerable?"

"You'll like her. Valleen has a heart of gold, most of the time. She's a bit of a hot mess. Likes bright colored clothes and shoes and hair. That's why Florida is perfect for her. She looks like the sun coming down the street sometimes. Oh, I love my Valleen; closest kin I got."

"A hot mess, huh. How come I ain't never seen her?"

"She was in Bowling Green for years and just left her seventh, count 'em, seventh, husband. I didn't much care for him anyway, though he did work. Had that goin for him. Remember, I went to visit and that's when you got the hypothermia."

"Yeah. I want to forget that." She was quiet for a few minutes, then said, "You're lucky to have a sister. I got nobody."

"Gracie Gepper, ya got me, remember. We're best friends. Don't ya have no brothers or sisters or cousins, nowhere?"

"Things were different when I grew up. If I had 'em, I didn't know it, not for sure; had ta call everyone momma or sis if I was livin with 'em. I was just with people; never belonged ta anybody, and nobody ever belonged ta me. Had a mom and dad for a while, then...," She left that thought just hanging there.

Marge had that same feeling that she had in her apartment back in Louisville when she knew, no matter how scared she was, she had to find the courage to do whatever in the world she needed to do to save her friend from nursing home rigor mortis. She stood up.

"We ain't gettin any younger, ya know. And if there is somethin we haven't done that we wanna do, we best be doin it real soon. Hell, what's the worst that can happen, anyway?"

"I can think of a lot of things that could happen, but don't suppose that would be any worse than doin nothin," said Gracie.

They laughed, and walked arm in arm to the bus doors.

"Okay, but I got ta warn ya," giggled Gracie, "I've got me some wild things on my list. Oh yeah, Florida is in for a treat when we get settled in." Suddenly, with their bellies full and the tire repaired, they were both in a jovial mood.

Back on to the bus, Gracie went on and on about her list, adding to it as the day went on. "I want my name in lights. I wanna be in the newspaper, not the obits, mind ya. Line dancing – have ya ever done any of that, Marge? Get the heebie-jeebies scared right outta me and come out smelling like a rose – not like that smelly old dumpster we had to hide behind at that busin protest. I wouldn't mind to fall in love again, maybe. We can take some chances, not just lettin life catch up to us. Shoot, I just might want to swim naked – I bet your sister, Valleen, done that already…you'll have to ask her."

"How about Josie?" Marge asked. "Wouldn't ya like to see little Josie again, see how the young'un is shapin up?"

"I sure would like that a lot. Put a star, or something, next to her name. Top of the list before we kick the bucket."

"I'm so glad you're my friend, Gracie Gepper. We're goin to have a good time in Florida."

"Florida Welcome Center folks," called out the driver. "Thought you might enjoy a twenty-minute rest in air conditioning, and some of Florida's fine orange juice. Back on board in twenty."

"Well tarnation. Didn't we just sit ourselves down? I'm asking ya, didn't we?"

"Let's just get on up, and stop being cranky, or I'll take ya back to that old nursing home. I snuck ya out, I can sneak ya back in."

"Hush your mouth. Ya don't even want to know what would happen if ya tried to get me back there. Is that orange juice free, ya think?"

"Oh, mercy. Didn't know I had to go so bad till I stood up. Move over. Outa my way folks. C'mon, I'm in a heep of hurry." Gracie wasn't the first to get to the restrooms, but she wasn't far behind.

They sure enjoyed the free juice. "What'd ya have there, Gracie? Orange or Grapefruit? Ya go on over to the other side and get another orange juice and I'll go over here."

"That's so darned good, I could do this all day."

"They have some of the prettiest flowers out front I ever did see. I wonder if anybody here knows what they are."

"Ya plan on plantin some? Otherwise, no sense in wastin your time asking dumb questions of people who have other stuff to do."

"Suppose so. Probably won't plant any, anyways."

"Look at this. What do ya think about gettin in the water in a glass-bottom boat?" Marge held up the brochure for her friend to see. "Look at this picture. Looks like fun?"

"Maybe. We could moon some fish and no one would ever know, 'ceptin the fish"

"What if there was some scuba divers down below?" asked Marge.

They noticed fellow passengers heading back to the bus.

"Mind opening the door for me, Marge?" Gracie had a cup of juice in each hand. "Oh. What have we here? Are you fellas really in the Military?" She walked over to where two men in uniform stood behind a table of military-looking merchandise.

"Yes, "ma'am. US Army."

"Whatcha doin here?

"Ma'am, we're representing the Wounded Warriors by answering any of your questions about the program. We also have some items that also represent Wounded Warriors. Just look around all ya want."

"You're from Kentucky, ain't ya?" asked Grace.

He smiled a toothy grin full of good teeth. "Well, yes ma'am, I am. How'd ya know?"

"Marge," Gracie motioned her over to the side. "How much money we got with us? It'll make us feel good to do our part for those poor soldiers. Dig deep, girl."

They admired their camouflage wrist bands on the way to the bus, and Marge pointed out the pretty flowers she had seen on the way in. They laughed about the possibilities of mooning fish after settling in again. "Says here that they do glass-bottom boats in Clearwater. We'll just have ta look it up when we get to your sister's. This Florida thing is looking better all the time.

eight

The bus pulled into the terminal and screeched to a halt. Passengers were standing before the doors opened, and began gathering up their belongings. Everyone was looking real serious, now, in a hurry to get somewhere else.

"Is your behind numb, Gracie?"

"What behind? My legs don't feel like they even know each other."

They stood to stretch, like everyone else, but not in such a hurry. The doors to the bus swung open. Passengers lined up to move slowly off the bus. Not much talking was going on. Marge was thinking that she just wanted to lie down flat on her front-side for a while. They both had a whole lot of tired and achy to get rid of.

It wasn't long before the bus driver piled up their bags in front of the doors to the station, and they were waiting for Valleen to pick them up. It wasn't but a few minutes before Gracie started her usual complaining.

"Did you call that sister of yours? How is she supposed to know we're here, anyways?"

Now Marge was too tired to answer, she hadn't expended this much energy in years, so she shrugged her shoulders and looked at the road and waited. When the red convertible came to a halt next to the parked bus, Marge ran to hug her sister.

"Look at you, Valleen. You look terrific. Come on out here and meet Gracie."

Besides saying, "Good to meet ya," Gracie wasn't saying anything except to herself. "My, my, my," thought Gracie. "Never in my life. I'm not sayin a mean thing about Marge's sister, even if I have to bite my own tongue. Look, indeed."

Gracie looked Valleen over, top to bottom. There she stood, tight, white pants, bright green, loose blouse, banana earrings dangling from her earlobes, and matching, bright, yellow shoes. "And, please don't let her be a kisser...bright red lips. I ain't sayin a thing. No, this is Marge's sister, only relative she knows of. Looks like a durned fruit tree."

"Valleen don't want us crampin her style for long and that is just fine with me," Gracie said.

They looked around Valleen's place and didn't have a chance to light on one spot before another colorful piece of her decor caught their attention.

"This is my favorite chair," said Valleen, as she arched her arm over a sky-blue, overstuffed chair, while looking a whole lot like Vanna White showing off letters on Wheel of Fortune.

"Oh, Val, your place is so pretty." Marge clapped her hands together and was happy as could be.

"Marge was right," thought Gracie, as she plopped down in Valleen's blue chair. "She sure is a colorful lady." Valleen chatted on about her Florida décor of lemon and fuchsia and on and on and on. Gracie saw pink and yellow and every color in the rainbow. Marge was just looking pleased as punch to see her sister again, and thought everything was beautiful.

"Can't complain too much, yet, about your sister," said Gracie. "She's been a busy bee, gettin things ready us." Valleen already had a little two-bedroom trailer reserved in the Breezy Palms Mobile Home Resort Park for them to share. She even had her fella bringing over some beds, tomorrow.

"Sure hope ya don't need this much color in our place. Remember, I gotta live there, too," Gracie leaned over and whispered. "Hey, it just occurred to me, Marge. We ain't never lived together before. Hope this works out."

Marge shook her head. "We are in a new world now, Gracie. Remember what we said about livin in the fast lane?"

Gracie said she didn't remember anything about the fast lane, but wondered if they might need a car to get around. Something to talk about later, especially since neither of them had a license.

Gracie watched Valleen's red lips move for the rest of the night. She leaned over to Marge, "She doesn't seem to have to take a breath now and again like the rest of us, does she."

"Shh."

"Girls, I sure hope you like seafood, cause we're having shrimp for your first night in Florida. My fella," she arched her eyebrows, "is bringin it over in a while. In the meantime, I hope you like red wine."

"Lordy," thought Gracie, "I guess she wants to let us in on some kinda secret or something, raisin her eye-brows like that."

"Mercy," thought Marge, "she's usin the same kinda sign-language Gracie does.

Gracie was watching Valleen, who looked like neon crayons falling out of the box; bright yellow pants clung to her skinny legs, topped by a flowing purple, red and yellow top. Yellow and red earrings peeked out from blonde and light purple hair. Purple sandals on her feet, and rings on her toes. Gracie felt a little dizzy when she tried to keep up with her.

Valleen noticed Gracie giving her the once-over. "I like to change several times a day, Hon. I just hate the sweat, you know." Valleen fanned herself with her hands to emphasize the point, which caused her wrist bangles to jingle.

The long trip and numb behinds were nearly forgotten by the time the second bottle of red wine was uncorked. Gracie and Marge both scrunched up their faces at the little gray shrimp, but didn't say much; except, of course, for when Gracie started with, "Ya know what those things look like?"

"Shh," Marge whispered. "Don't want to hurt Fred's feelins."

"Then he oughtn't take it personal."

By the time they met Valleen's Fred, ate his shrimp - they were pink when they ate them - and drank more wine, the girls were done in. Valleen showed them to her bedroom and said she would be back in the morning for breakfast.

"Big day, tomorrow," yelled Valleen as she left. "Welcome to St. Pete."

Gracie and Marge barely had their heads just right on the pillows, and said their first goodnights in Florida, before the music of the night was of two friends, blissfully snoring like freight trains.

nine

Gracie woke the next morning to the wonderful aroma of coffee in the air and sunshine that seemed to be coming from every direction. She was stretching and making morning noises when she heard Valleen tapping on the half-open door.

"How'd you sleep, honey?" asked Valleen, as she pushed a cup of black coffee in front of Gracie. "Margie said you liked it straight. She's having breakfast by the pool. Wanna join her?"

Valleen was as perky in the morning as she'd been the night before. Gracie closed her eyes, and Valleen did indeed sound a little bit like her sister. She rolled out of bed. "Thanks Val. The coffee smells real good." She slid on her house shoes and went out to find the pool. She didn't bother to change out of her pajamas.

Marge was sitting in a chair next to the pool with her head back and facing the morning sun. Her two hands around her coffee mug. She lazily opened one eye to look their way and smiled.

"Whatcha think, Gracie? Ain't this all just too beautiful? I think I'm in heaven. Our own pool. Do ya like ta swim? I don't think that topic ever came up before, did it?" Then she closed her eye again and continued smiling.

"Hmph,"said Gracie, as she looked around the grounds of their new home. They were waiting for Berle, their new landlady, to bring the keys and for Fred to bring some furniture from his used furniture store. They hadn't seen the inside of their place yet.

"So, Margie told me you two need to get to a bank to cash your checks, didn't have time to cash them before you left Louisville. Sort of in a hurry, weren't you?" Vallen giggled and patted Marge on her shoulder. "I sure enough can run you two newbies up there as soon as you're ready," bubbled Valleen.

After enjoying coffee around the pool, they got ready for their first ride with Valleen. Gracie had her purse that she had held close the whole trip. "C'mon Marge," Gracie yelled as she headed out the door of Valleen's place. "Your sister is honkin her horn."

"Oh, my goodness," said Marge.

Both girls stared wide-eyed at Val's neighborhood vehicle, a bright red golf cart shaded by a red and white striped canopy with red and white tassels dangling from it. Gracie pushed Marge to the front with Val and was pleased as punch to have the back seat to herself. She plopped down in the middle of the seat and grabbed the bars to hold on to.

"Let's get this contraption goin. I ain't never been in one of these before," she said.

Val was proud of her golf-cart. "Fred got it for a real steal. I love it." Marge filed that information away for later. Neither of them could look around much for gripping the side bars of the cart all the way.

Gracie listened and watched the two sisters in the front, obviously happy to be together again. "Wonder if I have a sister somewhere?" Gracie thought. "Guess Marge is the closest I'll ever get to havin family; reckon she will do just fine." Gracie didn't want to admit to the little pangs of jealousy she felt when she heard them up front talking and laughing. She reckoned that was what sisters did.

After a white-knuckled, jaw-clinching ride in Valleen's speedy little golf cart, they sat in front of the bank. Marge was a little scared about going in to the bank and handing over her check for cashing. It hadn't been all that long since she had kidnapped Gracie from the nursing home. She felt like a criminal, even if she wasn't sorry for saving her friend.

"I don't wanna go ta jail; I really don't wanna go ta jail," she whispered outside the entrance to the bank. She was trembling and near tears.

Gracie put her right hand on her hip, and scrunched up her face at Marge.

"Girl, I told ya that ya worry too much. Haven't I told ya that before? Let me go first. They sure-as shootin ain't gonna lock me up for bein kidnapped. If nothin happens ta me, you're in the clear."

Gracie barged through the doors like she owned the place. Marge followed, keeping a little distance between them. Gracie marched right up to the window, looking full of confidence.

But, when she reached into her purse for her check, she pulled out a half-eaten banana. Gracie barely skipped a beat. She looked at that half banana like she was glad to see it, told the cashier that it reminded her of kindness and good people, finished eating it, then put the peel back in her purse. Then she slid her check on to the counter, met the teller's wide-eyes with a toothless smile and said, "Cash this, honey. I'm in an awful hurry."

Later that day, Gracie got around to asking Marge about her and Valleen growing up together, like she had been thinking about it a lot.

"Aw, we weren't even close back then, Gracie. Just always knew we should stick together and be family, no matter what. Ya might'a noticed me and Valleen ain't much alike," Marge elbowed Gracie's ribs gently.

Gracie chuckled at that. "Yep, I did notice that."

And the conversation was over. Gracie was satisfied that there was enough room in Marge's life for her, even though Marge's sister was nearby.

ten

They both walked through the mobile-home-that-isn't-going-anywhere, and looked it over room by room.

"Fred turns out to be an okay guy. Pretty darn helpful, don't ya think?" Marge asked.

"Can't say nothin bad about the man. He must really like Valleen to just give us all this furniture. You don't think he's goin to force us to pay for this if Valleen dumps him, do ya?"

"You say the darnedest things sometimes, Gracie."

"Well, I ain't signin no papers for him."

Marge put away the few dishes Valleen had loaned them. Gracie was busy trying out the furniture and finally declared each piece doable.

"Wow, can you believe all this stuff? A light wood table with two chairs, blue and white livin room furniture, two beds and two dressers. What more do we need?" Marge was so excited. "I think this is goin to work out good for all of us. I sure do."

"Yep, pretty amazin. Nothin matches, but that kind of stuff never bothered me none," said Gracie. "Maybe we should buy some curtains to tone down some of these colors."

"And, we need our own chairs for outside our door, on our cute little patio."

"It's little, alright."

"C'mon Gracie, admit you love it here. It's warm every day and you look healthier than I've ever seen you; and we've only been here one full day. Shoot, you even look a teeny bit younger. How about me?" Marge batted her eyes, she was feeling sort of giggly.

"Aw, get on with yourself, Marge. I'm still a crabby, wrinkly, old woman. I do feel better than I did in that stinky prison. Did I ever thank ya for kidnappin me? I sure do appreciate that, I surely do."

Gracie started giggling and couldn't stop. By the time she was laughing out loud, Marge could barely hold herself up while holding her stomach and laughing even louder. They both crashed on the couch together and laughed till tears dripped from their faces and down their necks.

"Oh, my gawd," Gracie moaned and laughed and swiped the wet with the back of her hand. "We ain't never talked about all that. All I could see, Marge, was the other side of those doors and the blue sky out there, and the cab to freedom. It sure felt good to break out of there, Missy. What I do know is that fella that stepped out in front of us sure played his cards right."

They laughed even louder, wiping away happy tears.

"Oh Gracie, I've been just too scared to mention it. Now, it does seem awful funny. It would make a funny movie, wouldn't it?

"Yeah." Now Gracie had the hiccups. "I'd pay to see - hiccup - that at the movies."

"I'm still a little scared the police or old lady Harbo are goin ta come after me."

"No," Gracie patted her shoulder, "I think we're in a good, safe place now. We're okay, Marge."

eleven

They'd done their homework. After a somewhat interesting bus ride to the track, the girls found themselves standing at the entrance to the Derby Lane Dog Racing track in St. Pete.

"Well, Gracie, does this bring back memories?"

"Of what?" Gracie asked.

"You know, old times, that good-lookin guy you were in love with, way back when."

"Shoot, that wasn't nothin. We wasn't actually in love. Just havin a good time. Ya know."

"I see," Marge said. "Well, I guess I misunderstood the whole thing. Why don't we just get in there and check it out."

"What's wrong with ya, now?"

"Really? What's wrong with me? I thought this whole dog race trip was so ya could re-live a lost-love thingy. Now ya say it ain't so, at all. I don't even like dogs."

"I never said no such thing. I wasn't in love with that old bag of bones. Good grief!"

Gracie could see that Marge was miffed. She wanted today to be a fun time, so she had to make amends, somehow.

"Tell ya what, Marge. To make it up to ya, I'll buy ya a giant pretzel. How's that?" asked Gracie.

"Oh, I love those pretzels, and a lot of salt and mustard. Let's go."

The smell of hotdogs and beer and every other kind of race-track-food smell was everywhere. Gracie ordered a pretzel with mustard and two beers in plastic cups.

They found seats and waited for the first race to start. Marge looked over at Gracie when she heard her mumbling.

"Goin to the dogs. Goin to the dogs."

Marge didn't ask. Just ate her pretzel and sipped her beer. Marge enjoyed looking around at all the people and things going on around them. By the time the first race started, most of the seats were filled. They tried to study the guide for betting properly, but didn't learn much. So, they listened to people around them in case someone had a hot tip.

"I feel like I'm at Churchill Downs, just the horses ain't so big. Isn't it exciting?"

"Yeah. It'll be more exciting when we start bettin," said Gracie. "Let's head over to the windows."

Turned out it just seemed easier to bet the same amount of money on the same dog number for every race and share any winnings. They were both satisfied with that plan. "That's exactly what I do for the horses. I'm just happy as apple pie today. We are already havin a great time. Don't ya think?"

"Sure enough do," said Gracie.

"Those dogs are pure handsome. And they run like they love it. I can hardly wait to tell Valleen about all this. She'll want to come with us next time."

"What in the Sam hill …!"

Gracie turned to face the man directly behind her and swatted him on the arm a bunch of times while he apologized for spilling his beer that splattered on her legs and feet.

"Mam, Mam, I'm so sorry. Didn't mean to. Did it get on you?"

"What do ya think, ya dimwit? I'm soaked. Tarnation, my feet are all wet."

"Please, how can I make it up to you? Can I get you something? Really, anything."

Gracie looked at Marge and asked, "What do ya think? How can he make it up to us?"

"Well, he could buy us a beer and hotdog, I guess."

Gracie turned to look at him, again. She raised her eyebrows as high as they could go and just stared, until he got the point.

"Oh, okay. Be right back with beer and hotdogs." And he did.

When he returned, an unforgiving Gracie said, "Now ya can move behind someone else. I don't trust ya behind me. Go on. Git."

And he did.

Both girls enjoyed the beer and hotdogs and cheered for those greyhounds like they were big spenders. A fifty-cent or dollar win got the same loud response that a hundred dollars would have if that had actually happened. They counted and divided the small winnings and pretty much smiled all the way home.

"Have ya ever noticed how excitin things happen to us, all the time?"

"That's just the way we roll," answered Gracie.

Valleen lost all her sophistication when she blew her wine through her nose and out her mouth. She jumped from her lawn chair and ran to the bathroom to clean her face and wipe off mascara running from the tears in her eyes. She was still laughing loud enough for the others outside to hear her.

Fred was rocking back and forth, raising his feet off the ground and putting them back. His rocking was so even that he looked like he could have been in a rocker. Then he started snorting as he laughed.

"Oh, oh, oh," he cried out as he rocked, and snorted and held his belly. "Say it didn't happen. You've got to be pulling my leg," he cried out between snorts.

"If I felt like pullin somebody's leg, it would be someone better lookin than you, Fred," returned Gracie."

Marge started up with snickering. She couldn't hold laughter in when others were having so much fun.

"It ain't all that funny, Y'all. I could'a died today and you sit there laughin your fool heads off," grumbled Gracie.

Valleen returned to her chair with a cleaner face and a fresh shirt, but still out of control.

"Tell me again," sliding the words out with her exaggerated drawl. "I think I might have missed some of that story. And what in the world were you two doin way over there, anyways? Oh, my stomach hurts from laughin so hard." She bent over to make her point.

"Gracie's right, she could've been killed fallin into that dumpster head first. Of, course, I could'a died too, or worse, when I tried to help her out of that mess. Whew! It stunk ta high heaven, and…" she had to stop and wipe away the tears from trying not to laugh, again.

"Girl, it wasn't that bad, just a little stinky is all." Gracie has a penchant for being a little disagreeable whenever she can. Then Gracie did a little soft snorting of her own. "You were the funny one, trying to pretend everthin was hunky-dory while I had mustard, and lord knows what else, drippin from my hair. Man, oh man, that shower was a blessin today, I tell ya."

"That's not the first time we had a run in with a smelly dumpster. We'll have to tell ya that one some other day," said Marge.

"Anyways, there I am, tryin to put mustard on my pretzel, when some sleazy character grabbed hold of my bag and started runnin. Right there at the concessions, in front of thousands of people, though not many seemed to notice what was happenin. When I threw my pretzel and hit him on top of his head, he tripped, then threw my bag into a dumpster."

"It really wasn't a very big dumpster, maybe just a large trash can." Marge was trying to get a fresh picture of the whole ordeal in her head. Gracie wasn't having it though – had to be a dumpster, for her.

"It was a dumpster, no matter the size. So, I got mustard all over me, and I have to get my bag. Thing is, this thing was on wheels and I fell right in to it. Pure disgustin, don't think it wasn't."

"Honey, that's awful. What'd you do about the mustard and who knows what?" Valleen was being very sympathetic. She's known for being sweet.

"A few wet paper towels did the job, till I got back here. No big deal."

Fred was still trying to stop what, by now, sounded like giggling. "I'm sure glad you girls moved down here. You have me in stitches every time I'm around you. How do you get into so many messes? Don't you just love'em, Valleen, honey?"

"Sure do, babe."

She poured more wine into everyone's glass. "Honestly, you two are a perfect pair. So much alike. You're a hoot, that's for sure. But you got to tell us the whole story. I went over to your place bright and early this mornin, around ten, wasn't it Fred? And you two were nowhere to be found."

"Well, the truth of the matter is, we was already on a bus and on our way to the races."

"What races?" asked Valleen. She is not a sports kind of person, even if she does watch baseball now and again. Says she likes the uniforms.

"What do ya think? The greyhounds, the dogs," said Gracie, not sure if Valleen knew much about anything.

Valleen, feeling a little smarted, came back with, "Could'a been horses."

"Oh, I love the horses," chimed in Marge. "The only thing I miss about leavin my apartment, in Louisville, is bein right across from the racetrack. Gotta check on when the horses run here."

"Ok, ok," interrupted Fred. "Let's get back to today. What happened to you two, today?" Fred heard himself sounding huffy and confessed, "Sorry ladies, I sorta have a tendency to get a little irritated when people get off track, especially when I'm interested in the topic, as I am now. So, let's get on with it, okay."

Gracie, not in the habit of taking smart talk lightly, leaned in Fred's direction with a scowl on her face. She narrowed her eyes at him and tightened her mouth, which made that bottom lip jut out. But, before she could let go a word, Fred was apologizing again, hands out in front of him as if getting ready to protect himself.

"Sorry, sorry. That was rude. Won't do it again. Just meant that I really want to know what happened. Don't take me so serious most of the time. Okay?"

"We've been investigatin the dog race situation as Gracie was really wantin to go back again," started Marge.

"You've lived in Florida before?" asked Valleen.

Gracie heaved a deep sigh, and puffed out her cheeks. "I'd like to be done with this story someday."

"Long ago," Marge answered for Gracie. "That was all about some guy, but that didn't turn out so good. But that's another story, too."

"So," sighed Gracie, "we took the bus to the dog races, you know, the greyhounds. Went to the Derby Lane Track. Ain't like it used to be. The track is all fancied up, now."

"Tell them about the bus ride, Gracie. That was something else. You won't believe this story," said Marge.

"Oh, I think I'll believe anything you tell me," said Fred.

"Me, too," said Valleen. "Anything. Seems you two always come out of everything smellin like roses."

"Well," Marge said. "This creepy guy, youngish little snot, tried to grab my purse just before he jumped off the bus."

"We were sittin there right by the back door, ya know," added Gracie. "Who would've ever thought that we would get mugged twice in one day? Honestly, has anyone ever heard of such? Do we look like easy marks cause we're old?"

"Yeah. But Gracie was on him like a rat on cheese. She walloped him up side his head with that Greyhound bus bag of hers and knocked him clear off that bus. He fell right on the sidewalk, then got up and ran for his life. You should've seen it."

"Then Gracie chased him for a bit, yelling, 'You nasty thug, pickin on old people. Shame on ya.' "

"Oh, my gawd," said Valleen. "Really? You are a tough bird, Gracie."

"Yeah, I don't want you to get mad at me," said Fred.

"Well," said Gracie, trying to hold back a laugh. "It helped that we'd packed a lunch and two can sodas." They all laughed. Valleen was wiping tears again. Fred was hooting. Gracie and Marge looked proud of their adventurous tale.

"Let me tell you a story I heard about a greyhound dog, and I think it is the honest truth," said Fred, still laughing while talking. "This fella I know had him one of them greyhounds. Got it from a rescue group. You know, after the dogs quit racin. Anyways, my friend had an in-ground pool…"

"You want some wine, Sweetie?"

"Sure thing. Thanks, babe. How about a little more shrimp, too. So, as I was sayin. This guy is out there with his new dog and the dang dog walked right into the pool, like he didn't know the difference between concrete and water. Know what he did, then?"

"Swam!" Sounded good when all the girls said it together.

"No! He did not. That dog was dumb as a box of rocks. He stood on the bottom like he was waitin on a bus. The guy had to jump in there and carry him out. No lie. That's what happened."

"Well," said Gracie. "I think they are handsome animals, even if they aren't too bright."

"Yeah. This one dog was cute as a button and its name was Panflip. Ain't that too cute. I bet on her." And they talked and laughed till all were too tired and too full of wine and shrimp to talk anymore that night.

twelve

"Ain't this the life?" said Marge. Gracie didn't bother to answer. Marge was getting irritated. "I guess ya'd rather go back to Louisville where ya didn't have your own pool ta float in."

"Shh. I'm meditatin."

"About what?"

"Don't have to be about nothin, in particular. I'm practicing. But now that ya brung it up, I think I'm meditatin about how much I like bein warm all the time."

"Who wants to go to the beach?" Valleen was already in her swim suit.

"I don't know," Gracie said. "I'm already good and wet."

"Aw, c'mon, Gracie. We need to go out there and jump in some waves."

"Shoot. Last time I was out there, I felt like I was in a washin machine…agitated and wrung out."

"I'm in," said Marge. How about you, scaredy-cat?"

"I ain't scared of nothin. Just cautionary, that's all."

"Didn't you just say yesterday or the day before that we should get to the beach this week?"

"I ain't never said such a thing, Marge. You're makin it up ta get me to go with y'all."

Marge shook her head. "I'm gonna hav'ta start keepin notes if rememberin is gonna be my job."

The three of them headed to the beach. The flag was green, the water was just cool enough, and the waves were breaking nice and easy. "Sure wish I'd of grew up around a beach like this," said Marge.

"Me, too. That means we both would'a been there, sis. When are you two gonna get some swimsuits?"

"We're not as daring as you, Valleen.""We wouldn't look as good as you do. That's why. And, look over there. How can those girls wear such little things?"

"Gawd. Part of their swimsuits have disappeared somewhere."

Valleen looked at the young ladies. "If we wore one of those, we'd be ninety-nine percent nude."

"Nope. I think I would be more than ninety-nine." Gracie said, then chuckled.

"C'mon. Let's take a break," Valleen said, as she headed to the beach blanket. "Look, wine- coolers and cheese crackers.

"You'll never guess what we're gonna do, Val. Me and Gracie are gonna swim without anythin on. You ever do that?"

"Whoa. I'm not believin it. Really?"

"Yeah. Friday. Well, have ya?"

"No. But I am on Friday."

"Lordy, lordy," said Gracie, shaking her head back and forth. "I guess, the more the merrier."

"C'mon. y'all. Ya'd think Wednesday didn't happen every darn week. Ivy and Zelda will be wonderin where we got lost to.

"Don't be such a patoot," said Marge. "I've got the cards. And, you're not gonna miss out on anythin if we're a minute late. We'll get all the gossip we can handle."

Sure enough, Ivy and Zelda had the table and chairs placed near the pool.

"I've got the lemonade," yelled Gracie, when she got closer.

"I've got the cookies," Ivy yelled back.

"You make the best daggum cookies in the world," said Marge. "You should start sellin 'em."

"Not to us, though," said Valleen. "Anyway, have we missed out on any good gossip this week? Anything more on the new guy. Just caught a glimpse of him."

"Well," said Ivy. "You know we told you that Wilma was taking a lot of casseroles over there to him. And she sure can cook a good casserole."

"Yeah?" Marge was on the edge of her seat.

"Well," started Zelda. "She ain't the only widow around here. Seems he's been getting a lot of casseroles, lately. Just sayin."

"You have to draw your own conclusions," finished Ivy.

"These men are all the same, I tell ya."

"Except for my Fred, of course."

"Of course," said Ivy.

"Oh, I can't hold it in any longer. We're going to swim nude on Friday. Ain't that just crazy exciting?" said Valleen.

"What? Oh my." Zelda and Ivy were nearly speechless.

And that was that. The cat was out of the bag. The word was out there that anyone who wanted to swim nude could do it with friends on Friday morning. By Thursday afternoon, all the women in the park were talking about it.

"A few don't want to hear anything about it," said Valleen. "Don't pay them no never-mind. Just jealous, is all. They ain't brave enough to swim in their own skin. Not like the rest of us, ya know."

"Think about it. Won't it be all-that if a whole bunch of us are out there. What's that word…epic…thats it. We might even make the local news. Wouldn't that be somethin amazin?"

"No way," said Gracie. "We wouldn't be worth talkin about in the news. Ya think?"

"Why not?" Marge liked the idea.

Gracie was thinking about how that would be. "I'm thinkin about a walk around the park in a bit, to see what's goin on. Wanna go?"

"Sure. Wait for me to get some dry duds on."

So they walked. First person they passed was the new fella, who may or may not be courting Wilma. "Evenin, ladies." He smiled real big at them. "How are you two doin this beautiful evenin? I hear it's gonna be a little cool tomorrow mornin."

"Evenin, ta ya," Marge said.

Gracie kept walking. When they got to Ivy and Zelda's place, it looked like there might be a get-together happening. Ivy waved for them to come over. "Everyone is so excited about tomorrow." Ivy said as she hugged Gracie and Marge.

"What about," Marge asked.

"The swim, of course. What else? It's all anyone is talkin about. I get goose-bumps just thinkin about it."

"We're just swimmin, not changing the world. Are they swimmin with us or gawkin?" asked Gracie.

"Most of us are gettin wet. Those too scared can keep a watch out for the police."

Marge gasped. "The police. Why would the police be there? Oh, lordy."

"Shoot. I don't know. Maybe it's against the law to swim without clothes." Ivy grabbed Marge's hands. "Wouldn't it be awesome if we all got arrested? How excitin."

Gracie put her hands on her hips and puffed her cheeks. "All I'm sayin is, we're goin in at dawn. Y'all can do whatever ya got a mind to. And bring your own towels. Ain't nobody wants ta see your hind-ins in the light of day." She had a difficult time holding back a very satisfied smile, "Look what we started," she leaned over to whisper to Marge. "Pretty cool, if I say so my darned self."

"We have ourselves an interestin caravan," said Gracie, through a wide yawn. "Like a Christmas parade."

Marge watched all the lighted vehicles following them.

Valleen burst out in song, as she drove the golf cart to the beach early Friday mornng. "She wore an itsy bitsy, teeny weeny, yellow polka-dot bikini…"

"That sure sounds like your song, Val. You wear those all the time."

As the women arrived, they crowded around Marge, Gracie and Valleen. Everyone was talking at once.

"So, how we gonna to do this?"

"How do ya think? Just go in."

"We should hold hands."

"Good idea. Let's do it."

"How ya goin to hold your towel if you're holding hands, girl?"

"Okay. On the count of three, we run for the water."

"I can't believe I'm doin this."

"One. Two. Three!"

And just like the YouTube video later showed, they dashed in with no visible hesitation, like they had been waiting for this all their lives. Some dropped their towels before their toes got wet. Most, Marge and Gracie, for sure, wore their towels into the water, and threw them out when they could bend down to hide themselves. And Valleen, well, she was one of those early towel-droppers. You know, by now, what a hot mess she is.

Ivy yelled, "Hey, Gracie." She jumped up out of the water with one arm over her chest, and splashed Gracie in the face.

Valleen grabbed Marge and Gracie's hands. "Ring around the Rosie," she sang.

The women hugged and laughed like there was no one else in the water with them or on the beach.

Marge showed no fear of anything, free as the fish that lived in the ocean...until she turned toward the beach. "Holy mackerel!" she screamed. "Don't nobody sleep late anymore?" She stared at the people on the beach taking pictures and videos with cell-phones and cameras.

"Pretend they just ain't there. We're doin what we came here ta do, for cryin out loud. Don't worry about those folks. Hey, Ivy. You yell when you're ready. Okay?"

"Gotcha, Gracie."

"Fish," yelled Wilma.

A school of tiny, silvery fish suddenly surrounded them. "Darned slippery fish," Gracie said as she tried to get hold of one. They easily avoided all attempts from the swimmers to impinge upon their freedom.

"Let's go! Go, go, go," screamed Ivy.

It was a grand finale. The ladies waiting on the beach, ran out with blankets held up, side by side, creating a wall of privacy. The others threw out towels. And when the blankets dropped, thirty brave women marched, draped in towels and wearing sunglasses, waving at onlookers, all together.

"Hey, Freddie-boy. I saw you on the beach, gawkin, hopin to see more'n ya oughta." Gracie enjoyed picking at Fred.

He waved his hand at Gracie and he and Valleen both laughed. "He was down there to support my debut in the buff. You're proud of me, aren't you, Fred?"

"Sure am, gorgeous. You're awesome. Besides, no healthy man is gonna miss an opportunity to eyeball beautiful women in the buff. Right Ralph"

Ralph was the newest single male in the park. He hesitated to answer. "Uh, yeah. Sure."

"This pool party was a great idea." Marge wiped sweat from her face and neck. "I've already learned two line-dances."

"Never pass up a chance to dance," said Gracie.

"Gracie. Ya know what happened today?"

"Of course, I know. I was here wasn't I?"

"Ya done gone and did two things on your bucket list."

"Ain't got no bucket list. How do ya keep dreamin up this stuff?"

"I ain't dreamin. I done gone and had to remind ya before, that ya made a list of things ya want ta do before ya kick the bucket. Today ya went and swam in the ocean without clothes on. And tonight ya danced."

"Tell ya what, Marge, those were tryin times, back there. Whatever I might'a said, I'm havin a darned good time. If ya want, ya can write that list for me and I'll try to get'em all done."

Marge smiled. "Sure thing, Gracie. I'll do that tomorrow."

"If she remembers," said Fred.

The YouTube videos had been rolling on Ivy and Zelda's big-screen TV. Fred wrapped both arms around Valleen as they watched. "That's golden, baby. Just golden."

"Quiet, everybody. Turn the video off. The news is on. "There we are," yelled Zelda.

"I didn't know there were so many people on the beach."

And then the police showed up. Everyone stopped doing whatever they were doing. The music continued, but no one danced. The videos rolled but no one watched. Two tall, muscular men in their crisp uniforms walked right up to

Gracie. "Ma'am. Some neighbors are complaining about the loud music and partying going on here. Is this your doings?"

Gracie was stunned, speechless. Many ran to gather around Gracie. Marge ran over to her, wrapped her arms around one of Gracie's, and gulped. "No, sir. She ain't done nothin wrong. This is just a neighborhood get-ta-gether. Everybody's here. Who could complain?"

"Well, to be honest," said one of the officers, who looked like a younger Robert Redford, "that mean old man over there." All eyes followed the accusatory finger as it pointed to Fred. "We just might hav'ta cuff you, if you've been a bad girl," he said as he twirled the shiny cuffs around and around with his index finger.

Fred jumped out of his seat and turned the music up louder. It took the surprised crowd a few seconds more to realize what was happening. By the time the cops were swinging their hips to the music and unbuttoning their shirts, women were squealing with delight and the men were clapping and laughing.

Marge and Gracie looked at each other and back to the strippers. "Oh my gawd," said Gracie. "I'm gonna kill that Fred. I was plum scared to death. I need a chair and a drink." Didn't take long, however, for the girls to be clapping and laughing until the dancers had stripped to their speedos.

"Shh. Quiet, everyone. Listen."

"This is Doug Donovan, reporting live from St. Petersburg." He turned the microphone to a young man on the beach." What do you think about what happened here this morning?"

"Hey, I think it's great, ya know. Seeing older women who are happy with their bodies, havin a good time. Cool, man"

Then Gracie's face filled the screen. "It's no big deal. Just havin us a good time. Old ain't dead, folks." She waved the camera away and carefully got in the back seat of Valleen's cart and headed home.

The television flipped. Music played.

Gracie stood up in front of her friends. "Just to be clear. I never said I was happy with this old body. We tolerate each other, is all."

thirteen

The very next day the phone calls nearly drove Marge and Gracie out of the house. All kinds of people were calling. Somebody wanted to do a calendar with their pictures for some charity or other. A local radio station called to interview the 'ringleader.' Marge and Gracie were starting to feel overwhelmed by all the commotion. They denied everything. Most of the callers said they would call again, if that would be okay. Marge usually answered, "You can call back, if that's what ya want ta do." Gracie wouldn't answer the phone at all.

"Hey, Gracie, you think they might pay us for an interview? That wouldn't be so bad."

"I don't know what everyone is gettin all in a dither about. A bunch of grown women decide to swim in their birthday suits. Big deal. Ya'd think there was some real news to report, wouldn't ya?"

"Wait, wait. Maybe they'd pay us if we got an angle. Know what I mean?"

"No. I ain't got a clue what ya mean. I'm hungry. We got any tuna left?"

"We got plenty of tuna. I'm hungry, too. Ya want wheat or rye?"

"Both sound good to me. We ought to buy just one kind so's we don't hav'ta make these decisions every darn day.

"Lemonade?"

"Sounds good to me."

"What were we talking about, anyway?"

Gracie kept eating her sandwich. She wasn't any help, at all, in remembering with Marge. Marge finally remembered what it was. She got a piece of paper and a pen and brought them back to the table.

"Okay. Here we go. It's time ta write down that bucket list."

"Are you sure I called it a bucket list? That don't sound like nuthin I would even say. I can't hear that coming outta my mouth, at all."

"Maybe not. Let's call it your ta-do-before-ya-croak-list." She felt a giggle rolling up through her throat.

Then Gracie said something that was just about the nicest thing Marge could think of her ever saying, far as she could remember. "No. As much time as we spend together, we're liable to actually croak together. Let's call it our ta-do-before-*we*-croak-list. Ya know whatever I do, you'll be right there with me. Ain't that right?"

"Sure thing, Gracie."

So Marge worked her brain real hard to remember those things that Gracie had said she wanted to do that day on the bus trip. Marge thought maybe Gracie added some new ones, to boot, but she swears they were originals. Some of the things Marge wrote down, they decided weren't legal, so she scratched them out. Too bad.

"So, why are we botherin with this list, anyways?" Gracie asked.

"You asked me to make your, our, list so we could make sure ta get'em all done, sometime. Then we can mark'em off with a checkmark so we'd know what we did. For instance, we don't have to swim naked again, cause it now has a checkmark by it." Marge checked it off the list, right then and there.

"What if I want ta swim naked, again? Does that mean I can't, cause it's got a check next to it?"

"Course you can. But you don't have ta."

"Okay, then. I think I see how it works, now."

"Darn. I almost forgot the other thing. The angle. This list can be our angle. If we tell the people who call about our list, we'll be a lot more interestin to 'em, don't ya think?"

Gracie snored. Sound asleep. Didn't even finish the last bites of her tuna. That gave Marge more time to think about how to use that angle of theirs. "I sure like havin a ta-do list. Gives us some goals, and somethin ta look forward to. This is goin on our refrigerator, for sure," Marge muttered to deaf ears.

Valleen came over a little later to help Marge. She was like a jumping bean, bouncing from one thing to the next. She was helping make some phone calls, and finding the numbers for Marge. In no time, they had an interview scheduled with the local radio station that called them earlier. The angle that Marge was keyed up about seemed to work. Gracie was all heated up about the getting ready part, at first, but she finally let Valleen fix her hair and pick out some appropriate clothes for them to wear.

"Don't matter if it's the radio. You have to look your best for an interview," said Valleen. Marge was okay with some makeup and lipstick, but Gracie refused.

"Get that stuff away from me. You ever see me all colored up, girl? They'll have to take me as I am. Valleen, can you get a little wave over here, on the side for me? I used to wear it like that, a lot. Always looked real nice that way." Gracie watched Valleen work on her hair and seemed satisfied with the way it swept back. "There ya go. All pretty, just like in the old days."

So when the people from the radio station came the girls were sitting outside drinking tea. Valleen had been running around like a chicken with her head off, getting everything spruced up. She collected flowers from the neighbors, but didn't tell them what for. Valleen had a pretty flower cloth on her table that she brought over. "You did a real nice job," said Marge. "Ya could get a job getting people ready for interviews, if ya wanted to. You got that flare for fixin up, like nobody's business." That made Valleen smile, affirming what she had always thought about her style skills.

"Good grief," said Gracie. They were shocked that the radio people had a camera, and took pictures of all of them. Well, the three of them. Gracie and Marge told the reporter, leaning into the microphone, about their trip here on the bus from Louisville. They left out some details that they preferred to keep to themselves.

"I can tell ya all about our ta-do list," said Marge, eagerly. Gracie talked a whole lot more than Marge or Valleen thought she would. She really took to that camera and microphone. Whenever she talked she would grab hold of the mic until she was finished, and she smiled real big right into the camera. Good thing she remembered to put in her teeth.

"A person shouldn't wait till it's too late to do the things they wanna do. Me, I wanted to swim in the nude at least once in my life."

"What other things are on that list of yours?" asked the young reporter.

"Well, we've done gone and did a bunch of em. Tell ya what, I'll give ya a call when the list is done. Then you'll know what all we been up to."

The reporter laughed and said, "Okay. I guess I'll have to wait, then.

They were feeling like movie stars, with all that attention. Those were the folks who told them that since they would be on the news, and everyone thought they were so awesome, there would probably be some tourists coming by. The girls could hardly fathom that idea.

"We've done gone and created a tourist attraction... Us." Suddenly they realized that a lot of neighbors were crowding around behind them, especially the other women in the park.

"And, are some of these lovely ladies part of your swim group?" asked the reporter.

Marge, Gracie and Valleen had turned to see Ivy, Zelda, Wilma and the others, dressed in their Sunday-go-to-meeting-clothes. The interview guy smiled at the other ladies and said real loud, "Ladies, how about helping us out, here. Who wants to be on the radio and maybe television?" When he ascertained that they all liked his idea, he yelled, "On the count of three, all together, now, real loud, give me a, Go, Go, Go!"

And they all did. What a day.

Fourteen

So, after all the hubbub about the big skinny-dipping event calmed down, life sort of got back to normal. If there were any tourists looking for Marge and Gracie, well, they didn't find them. One really cool thing that happened for Gracie because of the publicity was that she was asked to play her violin at the retirement home not too far from their place. It's a real nice place. Everyone there loved when Gracie played.

Marge asked, "Gracie, would you mind if I sing some songs while ya play? I always wanted to sing for a crowd."

And, believe it or not, she darn well said she did mind, meaning that Marge could not sing while Gracie played her violin. Marge could hardly believe her own ears. Rejected by her very best friend.

But, before her feelings could be hurt much, Gracie said, "Marge, Honey, your voice was made for a piano. I'm thinkin maybe Valleen could tinker on the piano for you sometime to practice."

Marge has been working on that for a while. The lady at the retirement home said she could sing anytime she was ready, and that Valleen could use the piano in the cafeteria for their practice. Sometimes folks would come in and listen, but most of the time they were busy doing other things.

So, not much out of the ordinary happened for a week or so. Maybe, more. Maybe, less. Valleen talked the girls into going to some vendor-bazaar a few miles away. It was a good day to ride in her convertible, with the top down. They all had hats or scarves to wear just for riding with Valleen. She's not a slow-poke when her foot hits the pedal.

She loves her car. She or Fred were always buffing it up, making sure no finger prints or dust were on it for long. She wouldn't even let Marge touch her keys…not anymore, anyway. Can't blame her, if you knew the whole story, sister or no sister. Valleen isn't exactly holding a grudge, but she won't ever forget that Marge banged her car up a little bit. "Fred did such a good job fixing it up," said Marge. "I can't see the big deal."

So, to know the story behind Valleen not letting Marge even touch the keys to her car, it helps to know that it was Valleen's idea, after all. Marge hadn't driven a car in years and years. But, Marge also complained that Valleen made her nervous, and she jumped ever time she stepped on the gas pedal. And Gracie, she was in the back seat telling Marge to *step on it* and *ram'em if they got in the way*, having herself a good ole time.

And then Valleen yelled," Take a left!" But Marge took a right, smack into a stop sign. Gracie and Valleen screamed like they'd been flattened by a dump-truck or something. Marge screamed because Valleen and Gracie screamed.

Marge doesn't even like to think about that day, anymore. But, if for some reason it comes up, Marge will go on about it. "I was shaking from the highest hair on my head to my longest toenail. Valleen was pushin me to the passenger side before I knew what happened. Don't know why she couldn't give me a minute to calm down. It wasn't a good day, I tell you."

Valleen isn't the best driver, but it's her car, and it was a good day for getting out. Marge let Gracie sit up front most of the time since the front seat makes her nervous, now. The bazaar was really big, everything you can imagine and more. Valleen kept picking out clothes for Gracie and Marge that they wouldn't buy. They hated to hurt her feelings over it, but they just can't wear some things that she can.

"Don't you two ever get the urge to perk up your wardrobes?" she asked.

"Oh, Valleen, it's so pretty. It would look real good on you."

"I'm about as perky as I'm ever gonna get. If nobody likes it, tough stuff," said Gracie.

And that's the way the day went. Real nice.

They were plum tuckered out after a little while walking on the hot concrete. They took a break in the food area, after loading their plates with junk food. Marge bought one of those big pastries, with fruit and powdered sugar on top, to share and ate a juicy foot long hot dog with sauerkraut. Gracie had a brat and potatoes. Valleen just got a cheeseburger. After that, they were too full to shop anymore. So, they made a potty stop and headed back home.

"You two are fun to shop with. Just wish you'd buy something for the heck of it. Maybe next time we could get something to sorta match. Whatcha think?"

When Gracie saw where they were, she got Valleen's attention. "Hey, Goldilocks. Mind stoppin by the post office? I want to check for mail. Been a while."

Valleen swooped into the parking lot, and Gracie got out. She came back stuffing her mail in her purse, not even looking at it.

"Get any good mail?" Marge asked.

"Don't know. I can wait till I get home."

"I can't do that. You got more patience than me. Don't know how you can wait like that for somethin that's right there in your purse."

"I'm takin a nap," said Gracie.

Valleen talked most of the way home. She wouldn't let a person get a word in edgewise, sometimes. "Look in my shoppin bag, Marge. Get out that bright orange scarf. I got that as a gift for you."

"Oh, Valleen. It's beautiful. Thank you, so much. You are just full of surprises." Marge then unbuckled her seatbelt just long enough to give her sister a squeeze around her neck. "I'm a lucky person ta have the best sister and the best friend in the whole, wide world."

<u>Fifteen</u>

Gracie's eyes popped open as soon as the car turned into The Breezy Palms Mobile Home Resort Park entrance. Marge showed her the new scarf. Gracie nodded her head, and said, "Yep. Nice."

"Ya just don't appreciate high fashion. I'm gonna show this scarf to some people who'll enjoy it as much as I do. Goin for a walk."

Marge decided to head over to Ivy and Zelda's place. She made stops along the way to show off her new scarf that was wrapped around her neck. It was the nicest thing she owned and everyone was going to see it. She got oohs and ahhs from whoever she showed the scarf to, and she ate up the attention. Marge rounded the corner next to Ivy and Zelda's place to hear the ending of one of their favorite comedy routines.

Several other ladies from the neighborhood were sitting around their table, enjoying cool drinks and listening to every word from Ivy and Zelda, whose racy stories and jokes entertained all who listened, no matter how many times they heard them. Marge stopped so as not to miss a word.

"I heard…that you said…that my Carl…had a wart… on his, ahem."

"I did not say...that your Carl...had a wart... on his, ahem. I said, it felt like it."

No matter how many times she heard Ivy and Zelda's routine, Marge broke out in laughter and tears.

She ended up playing euchre with the gang for hours, especially since Ivy had baked some of her famous lemon cookies. "Dang! They're yummy," said Marge. "Sure wish I could bake like you."

She didn't know there was big news waiting for her or she would have walked faster, as she headed home. Gracie was resting on the lounge chair in front of their mobile home with her mail still in her lap. She was holding some papers against her chest with both hands, and looking nowhere in particular. Didn't even act like she saw Marge when she first arrived. That scared Marge for a minute, until she saw her chest move.

"You awake?" Marge yelled in Gracie's ear.

Gracie swatted her with the papers in her hand. "What in the tarnation ya tryin ta do, give me a heart attack?"

"What?" Marge jumped back.

"What, yourself. Why you scarin me like that?"

"I was afraid you was dead, that's why."

They both laughed.

"While you're up, why don't ya get us some lemonade? We got some stuff to talk about."

Marge had all the lemon she could handle after eating all of Ivy's lemon cookies, so she poured herself some tea, and Gracie the lemonade. When she got back outside, Gracie was sitting up on the side of the lounge chair, fiddling with those papers.

Marge thought it must be something monumentally important, or bad news. Or maybe some rich relative died and left Gracie a heap of money. She thought that maybe she should have opened a bottle of wine, and wished they had some champagne. Nothing to be done about that. They could always buy champagne later if they needed. Marge hoped so.

"Here ya go, Gracie. Did ya have a nice nap while I was gone? Ivy and Zelda wanted me to play some cards with em. Ivy's been bakin, again, you know how that is. What kind'a mail did you get, today?"

Gracie handed the papers over to Marge, her hands shaking.

"Here. You read it. Out loud, so I can hear it again. It's a letter from our Josie. Can you believe it? About knocked me over when I saw it. Go ahead, now."

Marge gulped a couple drinks of tea down, first. Then, she commenced to reading.

Dearest Aunt Gracie and Aunt Marge,

I am so excited to find out how to contact you. At least, I hope this is the right address. I saw you on the TV, and couldn't believe that I now know two famous people. I could hardly believe my ears, and my eyes, when I saw what you two did. But I think it's great. You two are a hoot.

I've thought about you so many times and how you helped me. I want you to know that I am still with Cody and his family and very, very happy. Me and Cody are getting married soon. I really wish both of you could come here for the wedding. It would make me happy, it surely would. And wouldn't it be great if you met his family, and could see what a wonderful husband he will be. He takes good care of me.

If it weren't for you taking me under your wings, this would never have happened. I don't even want to think about how badly things could have turned out.

Please, please, please come for my wedding. You can stay as long as you want. Cody's Momma said you can have the girls' room while you are here.

There is so much to tell you, that I will save till then. I am happier than I could ever imagine. I have my two favorite aunts to thank for that.

The big day is about four weeks away, on the 18th of next month.

Looking forward to seeing you, then. Call the number on the card, Cody's cell phone, and let us know when you will arrive.

Love, Love, Love

Josie and Cody

P.S. I can't wait to tell you at least one piece of news. I think you will be happy to hear it. I went to GED classes and now I am a high school graduate. Whoopee!

"Well, I'll be." And then Marge couldn't think of anything else to say.

"Yeah. Imagine that."

"I reckon we'll be goin?"

They sat facing the sunset, watching the colors change as small clouds rose out of the horizon.

Gracie took a long swig of her lemonade. "Wouldn't miss that for the world."

"We've sure enough been thinkin about that little runaway. Guess Cody turned out to be okay. I'd hate for ya ta have to teach him a life-lesson."

They both chuckled, at that.

"And she graduated. I'm right proud of that girl, I really am."

"Yeah. Me, too. Wow."

"Looks like we can write to her by the P.O. Box address on the envelope. Look, remember him talkin about that town of Valdosta? And, we have a phone number. This is great, Marge."

"All-righty then. Let's get to work on a letter back. This is excitin. When should we go?"

"Reckon we'd better check the Greyhound schedule before we decide on a date. Sure do want to see Josie, but don't think I want to stay in a stranger's house for too awful long."

"Okie-dokie, then. Let's get on it." And they did.

They wrote to Josie right away, telling her they would come. Just had to get tickets and such. So, after calling for the bus schedule and talking about what they wanted to do for several days, they finally made up their minds. They called Josie on the phone and she was real excited to talk to them. Her voice sounded so sweet, and her Cody got on and said he was so happy they were coming to the wedding. He reminded them that they were welcome to stay as long as thcy wantcd.

With both trying to talk excitedly on the same phone, they told him they would roll into the station in Valdosta on the sixteenth and leave on the nineteenth. "And, you be sure to not leave us stranded at the station."

"I promise. I'll be there waiting a long time before the bus is due."

"Okay. Now put Josie back on the phone," Gracie told him. "I got somethin real important to talk ta her about."

Josie came back on the phone. Marge had no idea what Gracie had in mind to talk about. She just had a real serious look on her face.

"Listen ta me, Josie. You're an adult now. And I'm as happy for ya almost more than I can stand. You're about ta be married and start your life with a good man. But somethin's missing. Ya might not want ta hear this, but I got ta say it. You need to give your Momma a call. No, don't jump in yet. Just listen to the advice of someone who never had the chance to call her momma. You have a cell phone, don'tcha?"

"Yes, ma'am."

"Okay, then. Call your Momma. Let her know what's going on. She won't know where ya are, unless ya want her to. Ya been gone a dag-gum long time. And ya ain't seen that little brother of yours, neither. Ya know he misses ya, real bad. See what's up with her. Give her a chance to say somethin. Maybe she learned that good-for-nothin ain't worth hurtin her family. Will ya do it, Josie?"

Gracie waited while Josie just breathed on the other end. "Aunt Gracie, this is real hard. Can I think about it and talk to Cody first? Can I give you that for now?"

"Course you can, girly. You're eighteen years old, a woman. Ya have ta make your own choices. But wouldn't it be nice if your Momma and little brother was at the weddin? What's the little tike's name, anyways?"

They could heard Josie giggle, as Marge had her ear right next to Gracie's. She must have felt good thinking about her little brother. Probably hadn't said his name out loud since she left. Sad.

"It's Rian. He is so sweet, and adorable. Mom's name is Jackie. I figured you'd ask that next."

"Maybe I would. Ya take care, now. We'll see ya soon."

"Bye Aunt Gracie, Aunt Marge. Love you."

She hung up. They smiled at each other. Marge had a knot in her throat. Gracie swiped at her eyes.

"Wanna beer?" Marge asked, as she opened the door to the trailer. "I need somethin a lot stronger than tea to wrap my head around all this."

Sixteen

Valleen insisted that the girls go shopping with her. "It doesn't matter what kind of wedding Josie's having, you gotta have new clothes." What surely surprised Marge was that Gracie was all over the idea of it all.

"I want to look as good as I can. We don't wanna embarrass little Josie, now do we? Sides, I'll most likely never go to another wedding in my life."

"Little Josie. Do you remember those long legs of hers? Never seen anything like them. Looks like a model, she does. Course, I want her ta know how proud we are of her, so, I guess that means we hav'ta dress smart."

"Good thing we already checked out the Goodwill, on the sly, because Valleen would'a had a fit. She knows that's where we buy most of our clothes, but dressin for a special wedding, and being like Josie's favorite aunts, has to be done just right."

So off they went shopping with Valleen. They weren't sure how a consignment boutique was any different from the Goodwill, but that's where they shopped. And Valleen knew where a lot of boutiques were.

"Come on out, Marge. We wanna see."

"If you don't come out, I'm comin on in," threatened Valleen.

"Ya'll laugh and I will be all over the two of ya."

They must not have been too frightened by Marge's threat, though. As soon as she opened the dressing room door, and managed to get all that pink chiffon, and all those ruffles, through it, they were both bent over busting a gut. She had thought it sure did look mighty pretty on the hanger.

"I knew I couldn't wear it to Josie's weddin. What I thought when I saw it was how pretty it would'a looked if I could'a gone to a prom wearin it," Marge told them. "I think it's beautiful. I might just buy it and find someplace to wear it. Then ya won't think it's so darn funny."

"Little sister, it's beautiful. And you would'a looked like a princess if you'd wore that dress to a prom or any dance. Wish you had." Then she hugged Marge.

"Valleen is sure okay, sometimes," thought Gracie. "She goes right ta the heart.

"Thanks, Valleen. You're a doll. But, miss giggles over there, that's another story."

"Aw, come on, Marge. Don't mean no harm. Ya know who ya look like right now? Gone With the Wind… Miss Scarlett… that's it. Big fancy dress."

"Really? Wow. Now if I could find me a Rhett Butler. I'd make sure he didn't leave me. No way."

"Okay, Gracie. Your turn to try somethin on." Valleen handed her a pink dress that she had been holding on to.

"I ain't wearin anythin that pink. Looks more like what *you'd* wear to a weddin." They didn't find wedding clothes that first day, because they got hungry and tired, and Marge said she needed a nap before she could do anything else. So they went home.

Gracie and Marge became so fearful that something might happen to get in their way of seeing Josie and Cody get married, that they were careful of everything. Like, for instance, they didn't eat any new foods, or get in crowds of people they didn't know. Stuff like that. Valleen just shook her head, but they weren't taking any chances.

"You girls wanna go swimming with me?" Marge looked up from her jumbo puzzle and Valleen was all ready to go, towel and all.

"Sounds good to me."

Gracie had just come out the door with two glasses of lemonade and some cookies that Ivy had left after they played cards last night. The girls sure beat their socks off, too.

"I aint gettin in the ocean. Some daggum shark bite my foot plum off and I'd be laid up in a hospital when Josie and Cody tie the knot. I'll sit and watch, keep ya company. But not long enough to get sunburned. Ain't nothin keepin me away from that little church in Valdosta."

Valleen sighed real big. "You're takin all this too far. Good thing that weddin ain't next year. You'd be hermit crabs by then. Come if ya want." She headed for the golf cart.

"Wait till we get our chairs, Valleen. And Gracie's right. Even if we are bein a bit peculiar, we can't take no chances. Not much longer till we're on that bus, headed north."

"By the way," said Gracie. "We ain't seen Fred for a while. You haven't gone and had a fight have you. I'm lookin forward to shrimp night, and that's tonight if I'm not mistaken."

"No. Fred would never stay away from me if we had a spat. He's too crazy about me. Poor thing, he's been under the weather. Says it's respiratory. He's stayin home so as to not make anyone else sick. He'll be back soon."

"Ya kiddin me," said Marge. "I can't imagine you and Fred bein apart so long."

"I take him soup every day. I just don't go in. Today he said he felt much better and would go to the doctor to make sure he's not contagious. Maybe shrimp night will be tomorrow. I sure am missin my lover-boy." She patted her hair and smoothed her swimsuit of a brightly colored explosion of pink orchids, earrings to match. "I'm gonna get some rays before I go to Fred's."

"Well, tell him we miss him, too. And ta not forget the shrimp." Gracie laughed at herself. It took a little bit, and she is so cantankerous at times that she hates to admit it, but she'd grown fond of Fred.

"Ya don't fool anyone Miss Gracie. I know ya like Fred, just for hisself," said Marge. She shook her head, knowing Gracie just liked to hear herself sound grouchy.

"I like his shrimp better," Gracie yelled after them, and had a little chuckle to herself.

seventeen

"Oh lordy, where's the tickets? Gracie, did you move the tickets? We'll never make it there at this rate." Marge was going around in circles. Suitcases were packed. Valleen was beeping the horn out front with the car motor running.

"Marge, the tickets are in your purse. Just sit down and calm down. What in the Sam hill are ya frettin about?" Gracie took Marge's purse, reached in and pulled out the envelope with their Greyhound Bus tickets to Valdosta, Georgia. "There. Mercy. Right where we put 'em last night. If ya don't calm down, I might hav'ta leave ya here."

"No way that's happenin." Marge took some deep breathes. "Ya wanna put them in your purse, instead?" she asked Gracie.

"Ah, no. I ain't gonna be responsible for 'em. They're good right where they are. I'll just keep my eagle-eye on your purse. Come on. Let's get outta here."

They got to the bus station with time to spare. As fast as Valleen drives, she's never late for anything. She swooped up to the curb at the station and stopped the car long enough to unload her passengers and their luggage. They all hugged, and Valleen was waving goodbye.

"Wow," said Marge. "What's her rush?"

"Fred's feelin better. It's been a long time…ya know. She ain't wastin anymore time on us than she has ta. Fred's waitin for her with a grin on his face."

"Oh." Marge was getting the gist of Gracie's explanation. Fred had taken longer to get over whatever he had than Valleen had thought he would. It had been a long time since she had any kissing and hugging from her guy. "Well, hope that works out."

"Imagine it will," was all Gracie had to say. She was rolling her suitcase into the station with Marge right behind her.

"Sure hope this is a better ride than the last time. Don't need no flat tire or runaways today. Just something about that Josie, makes me glad to be her made-up aunt."

"Yeah. Get the tickets out," said Gracie, as they walked up to the counter. The person behind the counter had little to say after checking their tickets. He pointed in the general direction of where they would go to get on their bus when the time came.

The bus to Valdosta looked just like the one they rode from Louisville. Same color seats. Potty in the back. They found their seats and Marge jumped in to claim the window.

"I get it comin back," said Gracie, as she sidled into the aisle seat. "I declare, I am as fidgety as I would be for my own weddin."

"Ya ever been married Gracie?"

"Nope. Have you."

"Yep. Once. I was almost eighteen. Had just graduated from high school. Never trust a jock, Gracie. They get treated like gods in school if they are winnin most of their games. They don't even have to show up for classes sometimes. My jock thought I was supposed to keep actin like he was all that, like his poo didn't stink. Know what I mean? Anyways, it didn't last long. He forgot he was married a few times, and I found out. Knew every one of those girls. Can ya believe that? Every last one of em."

"Yep," Gracie said, "I can believe that. And that's why, I guess, I never got hitched to anybody legal-like." There was silence between them for a few minutes before Gracie spoke again. "Growin up without a real family didn't give me a positive outlook, ya know, for that family stuff. And I sure as shootin wasn't gonna bring a kid into this world without a chance of havin a good family to grow up in."

They both settled in for the ride, first rooting around in their bags for travel pillows that Valleen had insisted on buying for them. Small blankets to keep their legs warm.

Grace pushed their compact cooler under her seat. Never wanted to take a chance of being hungry or thirsty.

Barring any unexpected events, they would arrive in Valdosta in approximately four hours. They could just barely hear music from somewhere on the bus.

Gracie nudged Marge. "I see a teenager. Wanna go see if she is a runaway?" Gracie chuckled. Marge ignored her. And the ride was uneventful, for a while.

Then a tire blew! Not as bad as when they were traveling to Florida, but a flat tire, regardless. "Sorry folks, looks like we have a little situation, here. Shouldn't take long to fix her up and get back on the road gain."

"Tarnation. How in the Sam hill can this happen to us twice. I'm not puttin up with it."

"For heaven's sake, Gracie, what can you do about it? We lived through it before."

She was fishing through her purse and pulled out a small notebook. "I didn't have Cody's cell phone number before. Now I just need a phone. Think I'm gonna get me one of my own real soon, too."

Gracie stepped into the aisle before everyone could get off the bus. "Anyone got a cell phone I can use real quick? We'll be late for a weddin if we have to wait on this bus to get fixed." She waited until the teenage boy, who had earplugs in his ears, offered his phone. "Thank ya. You're a good boy."

"Cody, is that you? This is Gracie. Me and Marge need you to come get us. No, we're not at the station already. We are in the middle of nowhere with a flat tire. Yep, we're in Georgia. Hang on. Hey driver. Here. Tell him where we are. We ain't waitin on this thing to be fixed. Last time we near starved to death."

"Way to go," Marge said, as she offered her hand for a high-five.

Twenty-five minutes later, their luggage was loaded into the back of Cody's truck.

Cody gave each of them quick hugs. He collected the luggage as the driver pulled the two bags out of the outside compartment. He was grinning from ear to ear.

"Sure is good to see you two. Everyone at the house is excited you're a comin for the wedding. Ya'll look great." He hugged them again.

Josie wrapped her arms around Gracie and Marge at the same time. She squealed loudly, causing everyone around her to hold their ears.

"You're here. You're here. I'm so happy I can't stand it." She hadn't stopped hugging them and was kissing cheeks when Gracie begged for mercy.

"Hold on. Goodness, Josie. A person's gotta breathe. Step back and let us see you, Honey. Look at her, Marge. Ain't she just beautiful?"

"She sure is. Pretty as a picture. Josie, you're a sight for sore eyes. I'm darned glad to see ya again. You're on our bucket list, ya know."

"Your what?" Josie looked confused.

"Ya know, bucket list. That list of things ya do before ya die."

"Are you sick?"

"Just forget about that, Josie. We're just happy to see ya again. That's all. Now let's get goin so we can catch up."

"Now, how's this gonna work?" Gracie asked, as she looked at the red pickup truck.

"I'll ride in the back. No prob," said Cody. "Josie can handle this old thing as good as anybody."

Marge and Gracie kept their eyes on Josie all the way to the house. She had so much to share with them, she talked the whole way. She talked about her new family, and how wonderful Cody had been, the town and the people. Gracie and Marge smiled. No one would ever know by the loving looks on their faces that they were pretend aunts, and no one seemed to even think that thought.

"Aunt Gracie. I took your advice. It was hard, but I called my Momma."

"Oh, good." Gracie patted her arm.

"Yep. She was happy to hear from me. Said she was worried sick and so sorry she put us all through so much misery. I cried when I talked to my little brother because he cried first. They'll be here tomorrow. I can hardly wait. Then they'll come back when my brother gets a break from school again. Some of the schools are doing that year-round thing now."

"What about you two?" Josie asked. "Are you happy in Florida? Seeing you all in the news was amazing. Never thought you'd do something like that. Just awesome."

"We love it there," chimed in Marge. "You can visit us anytime. Come to the beach. Maybe when your Momma and brother come back."

Josie turned the truck onto a gravel driveway. They could see the two-story house at the very end. Clean, white siding and sky-blue shutters, topped off with a tin roof. The front porch was overflowing with chairs and rockers, a few of them currently occupied by kids who were waiting for Josie and Cody to bring the first of the out-of-town wedding guests back to the house.

Gracie yelled out the little back window to Cody. "Watcha got growin out there?" She saw green plants as far as she could see on her right, but couldn't figure out what they might be. On the left, she guessed, soybeans. She had seen them many times, years ago. The house seemed to sit in a clearing in the middle of the farm, with a large yard and a rickety barn that showed no signs of ever being painted, and a few smaller out-buildings.

"Well," said Cody, with obvious pride, "we got us some soybeans on the left, there."

"Uh-huh, that's what I thought," responded Gracie.

"Yes'm. And on your right, that's blueberries. They've been comin in real good for about six years now. And, way out yonder, behind the house, we've got a great crop of peanuts."

Before he could say anymore, Gracie needed clarification on this crop choice. "Where's the peaches, and the tobacca? This is Georgia, ain't it?"

"Yes'm, it surely is. We've been phasing out the tobacca for years. Still got a little out there for local sellin. And we have peach trees, too, but mostly for the family and our fruit stand. You wouldn't believe what a good crop blueberries has turned in to. And soybeans. Everyone needs soybeans. Doin ok with these crops, we are."

By the time the truck stopped in front of the porch, a teenage girl and two younger children were all jostling, trying to open the doors. Marge and Gracie were both laughing and smiling and rubbing the tops of little heads, as the children were hugging them and all talking at once.

"C'mon y'all. Let 'em get out of the truck first and in the house. Geez!" yelled Cody. He never lost his smile.

"Land-sakes!" Marge was having a good time with all the fuss. She was hugging back and laughing. "Never in my life have I felt so welcome anywhere."

"Whew! They're like bees on honey. Guess I ain't never been honey

The kids settled down and allowed their guests to walk up to the front porch. That's when the screen door opened and banged shut. Gracie and Marge saw Cody's momma coming toward them with arms outstretched. She was a pretty woman, with a small build and a big bright smile.

"So glad you made it. Welcome, welcome, welcome." After hugging all around, again, she herded the kids into the house. "Get in there and wash up. Liza, put the chicken on the table, Honey. And get those biscuits out of the oven. I can smell them to be done."

"Your house smells delicious, Ms. Cleary," said Marge.

"Sure does," agreed Gracie. "I can hardly wait to get a hold of some of that chicken."

"Y'all call me Anne. I hope everyone is hungry 'cause we got enough food for a church social in here."

The table was set with hot biscuits steaming from the bowl that Liza had just set down. Fried chicken, mashed potatoes, greens and dumplings were waiting to be dished out onto the plates.

Anne folded her hands and gave a brief blessing over the table and people present. There were no strangers at this table, as bowls full of food were passed hand to hand, and plates were loaded. The younger children were giggling and poking each other.

Liza sat next to the younger children, keeping an eye on them and giving them *the eye* when needed. She had long chestnut colored hair in a single braid, like her momma's. She was tiny, like her Momma too, barely reaching Josie's shoulders

The younger girl, Bitsy, nine years old, had bobbed hair the same color as the other females in the family. She was about the same height as her brother. Her dark eyes twinkled as she looked at Marge and Gracie.

The young boy was Jonah, age 10. Like Cody, he had blonde hair and blue eyes. He looked at Gracie and Marge through his long blonde bangs. A bit shy.

"A good lookin family," thought Gracie to herself. She and Marge both breathed in the delicious aromas emanating from the hot dishes, and enjoyed taking in each individual, scrumptious aroma.

"You folks sure know how to eat right. Everthin looks delicious," Marge said as she piled dumplings on her plate.

"I'm learning a lot from Anne," said Josie. "She's a wonderful cook."

Cody chimed in while reaching over to hold Josie's hand. "Wait till you taste Josie's blueberry hotcakes. They are so good, I had to propose first time I ate 'em." Josie smiled at Cody just like she had when she first met him on the bus trip. Everyone else chuckled at his reason for proposing.

After dinner, Gracie and Marge sat with Josie in rockers on the front porch. The others cleaned up the kitchen, giving them time to reunite. "I'm so darned happy you were able to come here. It just wouldn't be the same if I got married without you two."

"Josie, Sweetie, we wouldn't a missed your weddin for the world. Looks like ya got a good family here. And Cody's a good guy," said Gracie.

"Me too, Josie. I'm happy for ya, I could just pop," said Marge as she rocked in the big white rocker. "I think I'm gonna need one of these things when I get back home. Forgot how good it is to rock back and forth."

"Cody's Papa made these chairs. He was a talented man. Cody takes after him a lot, his Momma says."

Josie wanted to know more about Gracie and Marge's lives in Florida and they wanted to know more about the wedding, so they talked non-stop until fresh peach pie and tea were served on the porch. Anne asked about the celebrity side of Gracie and Marge, so the story-telling and laughter went on. Cody's family was easy to be with.

The next morning, after feasting on Josie's blueberry pancakes, they all rode around the farm. The kids piled into the back of the pickup truck with Josie, while Gracie and Marge squeezed into the only seat with Cody. He was very proud of what his family had built and was determined to keep the farm successful. "Pop didn't live long enough to see the blueberries become our big crop, but he talked to me about it. So, I got them goin and, here we are. Blueberry farmers." Jodie laughed out loud.

Liza yelled through the open window in the truck cab, "He sounds just like Pop when he laughs."

"I hope our kids will want to farm it along with Jonah. Who knows? We have one of the most successful and financially strong farms going around these parts." He wanted to make sure they saw the peach trees and tobacco way in the back of the farm, before heading home.

When the truck stopped, the kids jumped out with baskets. Josie handed Marge and Gracie their own. "This way Aunt Gracie," called Jonah.

"This way, Aunt Marge. You and me will take this row," directed Bitsy.

Gracie and Marge were tickled pink to be picking blueberries with the rest of them, feeling like young girls for the moment. They ate about as many as they put in their baskets. The children did the same. By the time they got back into the truck, they all had blue lips and fingers. And, there were still enough berries for a heavenly cobbler for dessert that night and pancakes the next morning.

Cody and Josie left later in the afternoon to fetch Josie's Momma and brother from the bus stop. This gave Marge and Gracie some time to themselves and a much-needed nap. Before they drifted off to sleep, Marge said what Gracie had already thought many times. "Josie is in the right place, don't ya think? Ain't never seen anyone as happy as her and Cody. And what a nice family they have here."

"Yep. I think she's gonna be okay. Sure am glad she got on that bus with us, way back then."

"Yeah. We helped make this happen, didn't we? Well, I'll be." They fell asleep with their lips curled gently into smiles of simple joy.

Eighteen

The morning of the wedding was the start of a beautiful day. The sun rose to a display of vibrant gold and pink, with soft hints of myriad hues of blue. Eventually the sun rose higher and the blues prevailed, bringing warm air and a soft breeze.

Few of the inhabitants of the house saw those first rays of light and color. But no one could resist the aromas of hot coffee and blueberry pancakes wafting through the rooms where they were stretching and yawning. One by one, feet hit the floor and the house came to life, softly, slowly, as bare feet padded across the floors. Cody set the table, then gave one last bear hug to his wife-to-be before the others presented themselves. "I'm so darn happy, Josie," and he kissed her gently on the forehead.

"Me too. I've been smiling since the day we met."

Gracie heard the sound of laughter, and knew it to be the younger kids. The joyful noises put the first smile of the day on her face. She looked around the room she and Marge were sharing. Double beds where Liza and her younger sister slept. There was no definite divide of the room that one might expect because of the age difference. Two small rockers held dolls and stuffed animals. A few family photos graced the dresser. Most of their things were neatly put away before Marge and Gracie arrived. White ruffled curtains framed the one window that looked down on the family garden. This was a cozy room and a comfortable house.

She threw her pillow at Marge, who was still trying to avoid the light of day. "Ouch!" she complained. "Does that smell like pancakes? That could get me up. And coffee?"

"If I beat ya down there, I ain't promisin there'll be any left for ya," Gracie playfully warned.

Marge threw the pillow back and started her stretching routine. "I like this place. We're gonna have ta make blueberry pancakes at home. We can probably get 'em in a box." Gracie was dressed and heading out the bedroom door before Marge was out from under the covers.

Yesterday had been a good day for everyone in the house. Josie's Mom and brother had arrived on time. Josie took her Mom for a long walk and talk, where they came to peace with the past as best they could, for now. Her brother, Rian, became one of the kids very quickly. They played and explored all day and, again, after supper.

Anne and Jackie talked most of the night about the wedding plans. They had chatted by phone and email several times already about how Jackie would help in the wedding preparations. They, along with everyone else, would be working for hours today to complete final wedding preparations. The ladies from the church would be preparing most of the food, and a cousin was the official wedding-cake-maker.

Cody would be taking the kids to the church after breakfast to do a little decorating. Then they would come back to the house to get dressed for the wedding. Jackie had gotten Josie's permission to bring her own veil, the one she wore when she married Josie's Dad. Josie remembered seeing it as a child, and her memory of it was of a thing of beauty.

Gracie and Marge shooed Jackie and Anne out of the kitchen after breakfast by offering to clean up. "Y'all get on with whatever ya gotta do. We can get this. Go on, now. Ya both got lots ta do." Anne hugged them both and went upstairs. Jackie held back.

"Gracie, Marge. I want to thank you from the bottom of my heart. I don't know what would've happened to Josie if you hadn't befriended and taken her under your wings. I regret terribly that she couldn't depend on me, then. You are angels." With tears in her eyes, she gave each a warm hug, then headed upstairs.

"Well, then," said Gracie, wiping a lone tear from each eye, "let's get to it." And they did. Hustle and bustle was the theme of the rest of the morning. Everyone was tingling with excitement.

The bride-to-be was upstairs in her room with her friend who came to help with her hair and whatever else needed to be done. Jackie was aching to get herself dressed and ready so she could help Josie, too.

Marge was washing dishes and Gracie was drying. "Don't know where much of anything goes, so I'm not gonna try to put these things away," said Gracie.

"I declare. Ya sure can be a lazy-bones. We know where the plates and cups go, at least. I can hardly wait to get in my pretty new clothes, and get ta that church, and see Josie and Cody get married. I hope I don't start cryin when she comes down the aisle."

"Looks like you done did. Dab your eyes, girl. Don't try and get me goin, too. Ya just go on and get yourself dressed, if you're in such a dither. I'll get the rest of this. Not much more, anyways. Get on with ya."

From the kitchen, Gracie smiled at the sounds of the others in the house. Josie and her friend would be the joyous squealers. Someone, must be Marge, was in the shower. Voices bounced off the walls that would have been Anne and Jackie sharing their own excitement. "Good sounds," muttered Gracie quietly. "Happy sounds."

Inside the church family and friends rose from their seats as the double doors were opened by the two groomsmen. Bitsy came in first with a basket of pink rose petals, with Jonah and Rian right behind her, each holding a violet colored pillow that held the rings. They beamed, absolutely angelic. Liza and Jodie's friend, Kelsey, came down the aisle next, each carrying a small bouquet of violets and baby's-breath. They both radiated joy for the occasion. Behind them, Josie and Cody stood arm in arm, he in a new black suit which made him look younger, rather than older. Josie was glowing in her simple, but perfect for her, sleeveless lace dress. Josie wore her mother's veil. Together, they had gathered tiny purple flowers from the side of the house to adorn the crown. She looked like a princess. They came down the aisle to the sounds of the church organ playing the procession. Everyone stood.

There were ample tears during the service as the church was packed with family and friends. Gracie and Marge were trying to hold back the inevitable tears, but seeing the two moms pull out hankies was too much for them. "She's so beautiful," whispered Marge, sniffling. Gracie nodded, "Shh," afraid that speaking would bring even more tears for her.

No tears followed to the big hall for the reception, though. The groomsmen were spinning the Cd's. Long tables were piled high with scrumptious foods. Lemonade and tea filled large keg-like plastic barrels. Gracie and Marge were having a blast. They were introduced and hugged from one corner to the next and in the middle.

Everyone had heard about Gracie and Marge, making them near-celebrities.

All the single females, young and not so young, gathered in a frothy, loose ball of fabric in front of Josie as she prepared to throw her bouquet. Most of them were bent over laughing before it was all over.

Gracie and Marge were in the middle of the bouquet mob with Josie and Cody's family and friends all around. They watched as Josie, with her back to them, released the flowers. In slow motion, one could see a few petals drop as the pretty lavender ribbons waved in the air, making its way to the outreached hands.

But, in real time, the bouquet plopped in Gracie's arms as she tried to pull away, but not fast enough. She stared down with eyes wide, then promptly spun and flung them at Marge. "Oh no," Marge squealed, as she flung them at Liza. Liza "Eeked!" loudly, not expecting the bouquet to be re-tossed, and pitched them toward Jackie who re-pitched them high into the air. They landed in Anne's arms. Her mouth was wide open and she looked shocked. That's when applause roared through the room. Josie ran over and congratulated her. The Preacher, a widower, stepped up and congratulated her, too. "Looks like there might be another wedding sometime in your future, Miss Anne." She blushed, as he bowed with a flourish.

"Boy, that was close," Gracie said, then giggled.

"You scared me when you threw those flowers at me. I didn't have time to think. Maybe I should'a kept 'em."

Gracie headed for an empty chair. "I gotta get off my feet for a few. These dogs are tired"

"Aunt Gracie, Aunt Marge, Momma told us to fix you a plate of food. I hope you like it." They looked up at little Bitsy and Jonah standing in front of them.

"You are the sweetest kids in the whole, wide world, I hope you know," Marge said to them. "It all looks really good. Thanks a bunch."

"Why, thank you, darlins. How about you sit with us a minute, while we eat," Gracie said, as her plate was set in front of her.

"You make the best aunts. Me and Jonah were thinking that maybe you could stay here and live with us. We got plenty of room."

Jonah looked shy again, peering through his blonde bangs, but smiled at them. "Maybe you could sorta be like our granny's, too."

Gracie and Marge were momentarily speechless. Gracie finished chewing the one bite she had taken from the fried chicken. "That sure is nice of y'all, but we got a home in Florida. We'll visit again, though."

"And you can come see us, sometime. Swim in the ocean. It's beautiful. How's that for an idea?"

"That would be good," spoke up Jonah, "but it would be gooder if you were here all the time."

"Yeah, maybe you could marry Uncle Joe. He's so lonely." Bitsy looked at Gracie, pleading with her big, brown eyes.

Gracie was trying to think of something else to say to make the kids smile when she heard, "It's Electric!" "We'll think about it, though. Okay?" Gracie and Marge got right out there on the floor with everyone else, glad to be out of that uncomfortable conversation. Marge almost fell trying to mimic a younger person's smooth moves. Luckily, she was steadied by a nice-looking gentleman, who was in line behind her, and on she danced.

"Whew! That's some work, havin so much fun," Gracie said, trying to catch her breath.

Marge, too, was laughing and trying to catch her breath. "I love it. We gotta get ta dancin around the pool more. I think we'd have a lot of company, don't ya think?"

"You're makin me dizzy with all the things ya want ta do when we get home. What'd ya think about those kids? These people can steal your heart with all their sweetness."

"Excuse me, ladies." They both looked up to see the nice-looking gentleman from the dance floor holding two glasses of lemonade. "Thought maybe you ladies could use some refreshment after coming off the dance floor. My name is Clyde. May I join you for a few minutes? I need a brief rest, too."

"Sure," said Marge. He pulled a chair over, almost in front of both of them.

"Thanks for the drink," said Gracie. She had already figured which direction he was heading by the placement of his chair. After a few gulps of lemonade, Gracie stood up. "I need to go talk to Jackie for a sec. Nice ta meet'cha, Clyde." He stood and smiled as she left.

"Would you like to dance?" Clyde took Marge's hand and they were inseparable for the rest of the evening. Gracie was glad Marge was having a good time, but she knew she was going to have to hear all about him later, when she would be trying to go to sleep.

Gracie had finally spotted Jackie when someone touched her arm. She turned to see a weathered face, not bad-looking guy, built sort of stocky. "Excuse me, Miss Gracie. Remember me? I'm Cody's Uncle Joe."

"Uh, sure," Was all Gracie could think to say.

"Would you like to dance? I'm not real light on my feet, but I do my best."

"I'm not much of a dancer either, but I'll give it a try." She noticed he had more smile than hair.

As he held out his hand to her, he remarked, "I don't know about all that. You sure did fine with those line dances." Gracie could feel herself blush. "Tarnation," she thought to herself.

Settling down for the night, Marge shared something with Gracie that was extremely unsettling.

"I invited Clyde down to visit some time. He's so nice, and a smooth dancer, too."

"Invited him to where?"

"To our place. What'd ya think?"

Where's he gonna sleep? When's he comin? We need some kinda plan, here, girly."

"It's not a big deal. It was just a general invite. He said he'd love ta come down, but that was all. Maybe he could stay with Fred. He might never make it, any oh how."

"Well, ya'd better check that out with Fred. I'm just glad you ain't planning on him stayin at our place. I don't think it's big enough for that kind of shenanigans."

"Gracie! I wasn't thinkin that way. Only met the fella today. Good grief, why don't ya go ta sleep."

"Believe it or not, that's exactly why I got into this bed. Good night." Before she drifted off to sleep, Gracie remembered how hot her cheeks were when Joe complimented her and made her blush.

"Oh, and what did ya think of Cody's uncle? Liza said he's sweet on ya."

"Lord help me." And Gracie rolled over and pulled the covers over her head.

nineteen

Gracie was off the bus first, with Marge close behind. "Oh, look. There's Valleen." Marge waved frantically, as if Valleen wasn't expecting to see her. She forgot about the last step of the bus and tumbled to the ground, pushing Gracie into a crowd of teenagers. They were shocked, but able to keep Gracie from falling.

Gracie turned to see Marge writhing on the ground holding her left foot and crying in pain. Valleen was running to Marge, as were station employees.

Three men helped Marge into a wheelchair where she continued to moan. "Ouch, ouch, ouch. Oh, my foot, my ankle. Somethin's broken. Can anyone see a bone?"

Valleen followed in her car while Gracie rode with Marge in the ambulance. Once settled inside with a lot of attention being given to Marge by a young EMS worker, the girls returned to normal. "Dag, Marge. You could'a fallen on me and we'd both be gettin carted to the hospital. Ya gotta be more careful."

"Ain't my fault. Those durn steps are too far apart. I could'a killed myself. Would'ya miss me, Gracie?" asked Marge with a smile.

"Ya quit talkin like that. Sides, ya can't be that bad off. You're talkin way too much ta be too hurt. Ain't she?" Gracie finished by nudging the nice fella who was taking care of Marge.

"That's right, ma'am. We just need to get some x-rays. You'll be dancing around soon, I bet."

"So," Marge looked into his green eyes, "you like ta dance?"

"Sure do. And so does my boyfriend," answered the young fella.

Marge looked at Gracie and they both shrugged their shoulders. Gracie leaned over to Marge, not minding that the EMS guy was in her way, and whispered, "Guess we're too old to be cougars." And the snickering started.

"How's Fred?" Gracie asked Valleen while they sat in the waiting room outside Radiology.

"Fred, who?" Gracie didn't miss the sharpness of that blade. She looked at Valleen's face, which had taken on a hardness that she had never seen.

Gracie went in the direction she felt most appropriate for the occasion. "What did the old coot do, anyways?"

"Don't wanna talk about him, or it."

"Sure ya do. Ya been here all by yourself while we was gone and ya need to talk. When ya left us off at the bus station, ya could hardly wait to get your arms around that man. What in Sam hill did he do? Never thought I would see ya mad at him."

"I thought I knew everything about him," started Valleen. "Turns out, he's a liar, like every other man I've ever met."

"I ain't one to defend a man, mind ya, but Fred adores ya, head-over-hills in love."

"Hmph. Well, maybe he did, and maybe he didn't. But, he has something to do with that Wilma. They messed around in the past and he never told me about it. I can't forgive him." Valleen signed off on that statement by folding her arms tightly to her chest.

"Yeah," agreed Valleen, "people have gotten pretty sloppy."

"Hey, is that a new blouse? Sure is a pretty color on ya, Valleen." Gracie tried to distract her for a while.

They sat like that for a few minutes, watching people pass in various injurious states. Gracie, not usually one to judge people's fashion-sense, was amazed at the folks who came to the ER in their pajama pants. "Ya know," she leaned toward Valleen, "I can remember when a woman wouldn't go anywhere in public without wearin gloves and stockins."

"Speakin of sloppy. Just get it over with and tell me what happened, why don'tcha. Life is too short to play games that ain't any fun."

"Okay. You're not gonna let up, are ya?" Valleen turned slightly toward Gracie. "So. I go over to Fred's, thinkin this is gonna be a romantic visit, since he was feelin better. He opens the door for me all a smiling like nothing's wrong. Soon as he wrapped his arms around me, I got a hot flash. 'Whoa' I told him. 'Need to turn the air on.' That's when I saw Wilma's casserole dish on the counter. There's no mistakin her dishes, you know."

Gracie knew that. She'd never known anyone to have a whole set of bright yellow dishes, including oven dishes, except for Wilma. Couldn't steal any of her plates and get away with it. "And?"

"And? I think that says enough. We know why Wilma takes casseroles to single men. And for some reason, she thought Fred was single. Well, he is now, far as I'm concerned. Oh, you should have heard him apologizin for not telling me that he was seein her before I got here. And, tellin me that nothin's been going on between them. I'm wonderin if he has ever even been sick."

Valleen's face flushed and tears were in her eyes. Gracie reached over and squeezed her hand. "Sorry, Val. I hope this works out somehow. Ya know you always got me and Marge." to nurse her."

Valleen laughed a little. "Lotta good Marge will do me. We'll be taking care of her hand and foot. She's not a good patient. You probably ain't never had the opportunity

"Well, I think I owe that girl all the nursing she needs, so I'm gonna hafta suck it up and deal with it." They both laughed at that. Gracie wasn't through with this Fred and Wilma thing, but she didn't press Valleen for any more information.

Marge was the star of Breezy Palms. Most everyone, except Wilma, came by to wish her well or bring food. Ivy brought cookies at least once a week, even when Marge was able to hobble around with her big black boot and a borrowed walker. Valleen had all the time in the world to wait on Marge, now that Fred was out of the picture.

"Where's Fred? He isn't still sick, is he?" Marge finally asked several days into her recovery from a sprained ankle. "No! I can't believe it," was her response when Gracie broke the news to her, just as Valleen had told her in the ER. "Poor Valleen. I thought they were perfect together. I gotta go talk to her."

"She'll be over shortly, if ya wanna wait," said Gracie. She didn't think that Marge was resting her foot enough, but Marge wouldn't listen.

Late that evening, Marge and Gracie were eating apple slices with peanut butter while watching CSI: Miami. "Chemistry," blurted out Marge. Gracie looked her way but did not respond. She'd learned to wait to see if anything more was going to come of it.

"Valleen and Fred had chemistry, for sure. But I thought they had whatever the other thing is that makes a good couple. Didn't you, Gracie?"

"Yep."

"Good thing we don't have chemistry. It sure does muddy the waters."

"WHAT!" Gracie looked at her with her eyes wide open.

"We get along so good the way we are. If we had chemistry, ya don't know if we would end up like Fred and Valleen or Ivy and…"

"What in the tarnation are you talkin about? Chemistry? We ain't nothin like any of those. Do I need to lock my bedroom door, for chrissakes?"

"Wait." Marge was flushed. "You're not gettin what I'm sayin."

Gracie stood up to put away the peanut butter. "I don't think *you're* gettin what you're sayin!"

"I just was tryin to figure out what went wrong for Valleen is all. Are you mad at me?"

"That's your problem. Ya gotta quit doin that deep thinkin. It gets ya in trouble all the time. And I ain't mad at ya. I'll probably laugh myself to sleep tonight. See ya in the mornin."

"Nite Gracie." Marge didn't hear the click of Gracie's doorknob-lock. But, she did hear Gracie in there snickering.

The next day was another sunny day in St. Pete. "Marge, I'm goin for a little walk. Need some exercise," said Gracie, after she brought out some lemonade and cheese and crackers to keep Marge busy for a while. Marge was sitting on the patio with her left foot propped up.

"Want me to go with ya?"

"Back in a while," was Gracie's response.

Gracie found Wilma sitting on her patio reading her AARP magazine. "Anythin good in there? I like the articles about senior romance."

"Whatcha want, Gracie Gepper?" Wilma was on the defense, knowing how tight Gracie was with Valleen. She put her magazine down, so Gracie couldn't see the article. Gracie figured it must be about sex and romance.

"I like ya, some, Wilma. You're not a bad neighbor. But ya know I got to be loyal to Valleen, don't ya?"

"I don't really care one way or another. Valleen is a hothead. That's all. Got people talking about nothin."

Gracie sat down in an empty chair. "Well. Just tell me what's goin on. Are you and Fred messin around or not?"

"Oh, for cryin out loud. This is ridiculous. I try to do a nice deed and Valleen gets in a snit. Serves her right if Fred just leaves her alone."

"Ya ain't answered my question," Gracie said slowly as she leaned forward.

Wilma took a deep breath. "No. We ain't doin nothin. I just took him some chicken and dumplins. Heard he was sick. We saw each other for a while, some time back. When Valleen moved in, he decided he wanted to be single again. I'm the one should be mad, not her." She crossed her arms and looked away.

"Hey. I'm sorry 'bout all that stuff. Just want to make things right if they need be. That's all. Hey, ya know what Marge wants to do as soon as she's back on both feet? She says we need to start dancin 'round the pool at least once a week. Don't that sound like some fun? And you got all those cool Cd's. Whatcha think?"

"Well. That does sound good. Matter of fact, no sense in waiting for Marge. She can watch until her foot heals. What if I get the word out and we do it Friday? Maybe cookout, too."

"Ya got a good idea there, Wilma. Yep, ya always have good ideas. I'll see ya Friday, then." Gracie walked away from Wilma's, then turned toward Fred's place. She needed to talk to him, now that she had more information on the situation. She wanted his side of the story.

Fred opened the door after Gracie knocked. She was slightly out of breath after climbing the steps to his apartment. "This is the surprise of the century, Gracie. Wanna come in?"

She barely waited for him to finish.

"Nice place ya got here, Fred. I see ya let Valleen help ya decorate." Gracie plopped down on an overstuffed blue chair with big white flowers.

"Gracie, you know I'd let Valleen do anything she wanted. If she likes it, I like it. I'm crazy about that woman, but she won't talk to me, at all. Never saw her this way. Don't know what to do, because I sure miss her."

"That's why I'm here. Now, this is the way it's gonna go down…"

That Friday evening the pool area was getting crowded. Everyone was in the mood for a party. The grill was hot and several men took over the cooking. There was so much food that some of the men dragged plastic tables and extra chairs over from nearby patios. Tempting appetizers, salads and desserts of all sizes and colors invited tasters and double-dippers, before the main course of burgers and dogs was ready from the hot coals.

Wilma had volunteers helping spin the Cd's. "Hey, Ralph. Come dance with me." Poor, shy Ralph didn't know how to say no, so he'd have to dance with Wilma several times before the night was over. Wilma loved to dance more than anything, well, most anything.

Gracie had Marge set up at a table in the middle of all the action, with her leg propped on a cushion and a drink in her hand. "I'm goin after that sister of yours. She ain't goin to sit over there by herself and miss the fun."

"Good for you, Gracie. You're like an angel sometimes, ya know. Would ya get me some guacamole and chips before ya go?"

Gracie banged on Valleen's door and then sat in one of her chairs. "What in the Sam hill are you banging on my door like that for?"

"Come on out. I need to talk to ya."

"I'm not in the mood. Catch me later."

"Valleen. We are talkin tonight. Just depends on how many times you want me to bang on that darned door. And, bring me a beer."

"Here," she said as she handed Gracie a cold one. "Maybe that will cool you off. What's so important that you have to leave the big party?" She sat in her favorite patio chair, then looked puzzled. "Where's my table? Did someone take my table to the pool party? At least they could ask."

"Get out of your dither, woman. Why ain't ya over there with us? Ya love a party." Valleen huffed but didn't answer. "I never saw anyone so determined to be miserable for no good reason."

"By gawd, I…"

Gracie didn't let her get any further. "Ah no. You had your chance to talk. Now it's my turn, Missy. You're in a snit for nothin. That Wilma knows she doesn't stack up to you, especially when it comes to Fred. Y'all look googley-eyed at each other, day after day after day. But I gotta take care of Marge, and this whole thing about you and Fred is upsettin to her. So, I want ya to pull up your huffy britches and listen to the man so ya'll can get on with bein happy again. Understand?"

"Well, when am I supposed to do that? I told him not to talk to me again, ever."

Gracie stood. "No time like the present, I hear they say." and walked back toward the pool. She gave the nod to Fred, who had been waiting behind a large bush for his cue to approach Valleen, just like they had planned, and then walked back toward the pool. Gracie's work was done, here.

Before she was out of earshot, she heard Fred, "I really love you, Honey."

"Oh, Fred," Val said, as she wrapped her arms around his neck.

Gracie unlocked the wheels to Marge's chair. "Be real quiet and I'll show ya somethin happy."

"Ooh." Marge smiled in anticipation as her friend rolled her in the direction of Valleen's place. She loved surprises. "Oh, goody," and patted Gracie's hand. "They're back together."

They watched as Fred and Valleen slow-danced, cheek to cheek as Rod Stewart's sexy, gravelly voice floated through the night air.

"I'll leave it to ya to talk to your hard-headed sister about forgivin Wilma. No sense in waistin time on foolish grudges."

"Gotcha. Let's get back to the pool and leave those two alone for a while. They got a lot of catchin up to do."

twenty

They awoke to the pleasant sound of rain pattering on the roof, hard and steady. Gracie was the first to get to the coffee pot. By the time Marge sat at the table, toast and a cup of coffee were waiting.

Marge buttered and jellied her toast like a hungry woman. "Looks like one of those days, dontcha think?"

"Sure enough does. Guess we can piddle around in here, maybe get some cleanin done," Gracie mumbled with little enthusiasm.

"Yeah, I suppose. Ain't nothing wrong with a lazy day, either." Marge had gotten out of the ankle boot the day before and was antsy to do something fun "Know what we should do today?"

Gracie waited for her to finish, but eventually asked the question, "What do ya think should we do?"

"Go to the dog races again. What did ya call it? Goin to the dogs?"

"Girl, I didn't think ya really liked the dogs."

"Course, I did. Don't know how ya got an idea like that. Let's just do it." Marge had a satisfied look on her face like the plan was set.

"Well then, let's get goin. Get there early, we might mosey around and eyeball some of the dogs before the race." And that was the day's well laid plan.

The precocious little girl in the seat in front of Gracie and Marge, on the bus, stared them down the whole trip to the dog track. Of course that didn't bother them, only offered free entertainment.

Gracie whispered close to Marge's ear, "Watch this." Gracie had a knack for bugging her eyes out real big and thought that would creep the child out. She leaned real close, without a sound, and stared.

The child returned the look with equally bugged eyes and added rolling her tongue out from the depths of somewhere and touched the tip of her own nose.

"Darnation," responded Gracie. "This child is hard core, for sure." Marge snickered. The competition continued with Gracie trying to shock the kid and Marge doing funny faces. They fist-bumped the kid as they exited the bus.

"That girl must cause her momma a lot of grief."

Marge elbowed Gracie, "I bet she reminds you of yourself. Let's see what kind of trouble we can get into."

"Trouble?" Marge didn't like that word. "We've had enough close calls that made me nervous to the point of nausea."

"Shh," said Gracie. "I bet the dogs are in that there blue building." The blue building held supplies of all nature, but they found the dogs in a nearby building. They were all in cages. And the whole area smelled nasty, urine and dog doo.

"Aw, poor babies. You look so sad." Marge stooped down to coo at one."

"You sound like ya talking to a baby, for Pete's sake."

"They are like babies. Lookie at'em"

Gracie bent over to rub a snout. Her body wasn't made to squat like Marge could. "How ya keep yourself so bony, girl? You and that sister of yours. Ahh, this one is a sweetie, ain't she?" Sweetie enjoyed the snout-rub and looked at Gracie with her large wet eyes.

"It's terrible, them in cages like this. No wonder they like to run. I'd like to let'em all out and let'em run away. Wouldn't you?"

"Nope. Don't ya know nothing about the streets? Mean world for stray dogs. Let's git outta here."

The girls got their hotdogs and beer without incident, then found seats near the fence. "Pays to get in the doors early, don't it? I'll tell ya what…I ain't letting some sloppy beer guzzler stand behind me again."

"I just keep thinkin about those poor dogs in cages, especially that one, you know. I don't know if I can enjoy these darn races now." Marge looked pouty at Gracie as if she expected her to have an answer to her sad feelings.

"Tarnation, Marge. We can't go around letting dogs outta cages and such."

"Why not, I wanna know?"

"Lord have mercy on me. Let's go and look at em some more. Won't hurt none, I guess."

As they approached the area where the dogs were waiting in their cages, they heard men's voices. Gracie grabbed Marge's arm to keep her from barreling around the corner.

"I didn't know this was Sweetie's last race. Have you contacted the rescue people?"

"Hell, no. Got too much going on to mess with them. You wouldn't believe the paperwork."

"What do you plan to do with her, then?" The man seemed just mildly curious, as opposed to concerned.

"I got it covered. Simpler for me this way. The vet will take care of it for me."

"Mm," said the mildly curious guy.

"Did ya hear that, Gracie. Oh, mercy. They're gonna kill the poor thing. Pure mean of em, I tell ya. We're not gonna let it happen, are we?"

"Shh, I'm ponderin."

Marge could see her friend thinking real hard. Grace scratched her head and squinted her eyes like they hurt.

Then she wrinkled her forehead and screwed up the right side of her face and looked into a far distance. Looking for solutions. Then she nodded her head.

"How long did ya take makin a plan to rescue me from the hellhole they put me in?"

Oh, took a purty long time, I guess. Don't think we have that much time, do you?"

"Okay. We gotta get the dog, need a leash, gotta hide the dog, and get it home without us bein killed or thrown in jail. And, we gotta do all that before the races are over. Let's get to it."

~.~

While the girls shopped for rescue items at a close-by drug store, a storm, of such, was brewing back home.

Val had spotted him lurking around, puffing on a stinky cigar. She detested cigars. But now, he was standing in front of Marge and Gracie's place. "Is there something I can do for you, mister?" Her voice didn't sound the list bit welcoming.

"Morning, ma'am. I'm looking for some old friends. Last I heard they was living here in this trailer park. Do you know who lives here?"

Val knew he was lying. She didn't like anything about him. "Who you looking for?" she didn't bother to answer his question.

"Two ladies. Gracie Gepper and Marge Cater. Do they live here?"

"I live here." Valleen crossed her arms and glared at the intruder.

He didn't seem to mind. "Must be used to people not liking him," she thought.

"So you live here. Mind if I ask how long?"

"Yes I do."

"Do what? Mind or live here."

"Yep," was her response. She wasn't going to make anything easy for this troublemaker. She even followed him to his car to take a picture of his car plate. "I'll know who that bum is in no time."

~.~

The girls were back at the track well before the end of the races, after shopping for the items they needed to rescue the greyhound.

"We gotta be careful. This could end us up in jail," said Gracie.

"Ain't the first time we got close to the slammer."

Gracie scrunched up her face at Marge acting street-smart. "I sorta wanna keep it that way. Just watchin that Orange and Black show scared me straight."

"She's still here. What do we do, next?"

"We're gonna get her out of that cage and get this leash on her first. Get the bag of doggie treats and pass em out." Gracie was surprised at how easy it was to open the cage.

"That's a girl. We're gonna take ya to your new home, now. That's right. Gonna be a good little puppy for me?" The dog wagged its little tail and slobbered on Gracie's hands as she buckled the leash. "Keep feedin those dogs. We can't have any barkin goin on."

"Ya ready for the paint, yet? I ain't never painted a dog before."

"I reckon we could be the first at it," said Gracie as she shook the can. A few minutes later a mess of paint was all over the three of them. "Lordy, how we gonna get home like this?"

Marge had tried to protect Sweetie's eyes and nose while Gracie sprayed brown hair paint all over the dog for camouflage. They possibly were more camouflaged than the intended victim, but the dog was no longer gray. Even better, she looked pretty mangy.

Angry voices were close by. Marge grabbed Gracie's arm, "What do we do? Oh, dear?" Tears were welling up in her eyes.

Gracie looked from one area to another, looking for an escape. "There. I think it's a doggie door. We gotta do it and fast. You go first and get the heck out of sight with the dog. It might take me a minute. Go on. Git." Gracie watched as Marge crawled through the opening, fast as she could, on all fours, knowing there was no way she, herself, could do it.

"Who the heck are you, and watcha doing in here?"

Gracie was relieved that it wasn't the foul man she heard earlier. She could handle this one. "I sure am glad you're here. I quit this job, right now. The application said nothin about cleanin up messes like this. Oh, no. I don't clean up after a bunch of mangy animals. People are bad enough."

"What the heck are you talkin about, lady? We don't need no cleaning lady in here. Need nothing but a hose."

"Well, good enough." She threw down a filthy rag she had used to wipe paint off her hands. I'm outta here, then. Who do I see about getting paid for my time?"

"I don't know. Ask at concessions."

She walked as fast as her chunky legs would let her and didn't stop until she was out of sight of the building. She found a tree to lean against, gasping for air. "Oh...my...god."

"Psst. Over here."

Marge was peeking out from behind a large bush. And Gracie hoped Sweetie was with her.

"Lordy, girl. You'd better still have that mutt. I almost had a heart attack back there because of her. She made it to the bush and saw Sweetie resting in the shade of the overgrown bush. "She don't have a clue what we done for her today, does she?"

"I was so scared for you. I didn't know what to do when you didn't crawl out the hole. Then I heard somebody talkin mean-like, and I started shakin."

"We gotta get out of here with this dog and I don't know how we're gonna do it, so let's get going."

"How will we do it?" Marge was bumping her knuckles together like she was running on batteries and couldn't stop. "Oh goodie, you're ponderin again."

"I see an exit."

"Excuse me ladies. Pets aren't allowed in here." They jumped and turned to face a guy with a shovel. He looked the dog over as if trying to determine what kind of disease it might have to have such dry, ugly fur. "You'll have to take it back out to your car."

"This is a dog track and you don't let dogs in?" Gracie tried to sound offended. "Tell ya what young man. I ain't bringin my dog back here anyways. They wouldn't even look at her. I told em she was fast as lightenin, but no, they acted all uppity, and all. We're outta here."

~.~

Back at the Breezy Palms, Valleen had rallied the neighbors to help protect her sister and Gracie. Turns out, it was really Marge that detective was looking for. Nasty old landlady back in Louisville claims she owed her at least two weeks rent, and maybe more since she didn't give notice before she moved out. She still had to get hold of Berle.

"Who's there?" came from inside after Valleen knocked on her landlady's door.

"Afternoon, Berle. Need to talk to you about my sister and Gracie. Have you been out for the morning?"

"Just got home. Doing a little redecorating, need some things. Do you like this color?"

"Love it," said Val without really looking. "Gotta big favor, Berle." She sat down on Berles's green sofa.

"What is it honey?" She plopped on to her sofa.

"There's some dirty ole guy lookin for Marge, says she owes her landlady in Louisville money and that ain't true. He lied to me this morning about who he was. You know those two, they're just trying to live out their days in peace and they pay you on time every single month. These are just mean-spirited people. Will you help the girls?"

"Sure will. Do I say I never heard of em?"

"Actually, it's probably best if you said they were here but high-tailed it out, right after they were in the news. Headed back to Louisville, or somewhere up North. And don't mention that she has a sister at all."

"It's done." She patted Valleen on her hand. "So, let me show you what I bought today." Valleen already knew the consequences in asking Berle for a favor. It was worth the time, if it helped Marge and Gracie.

~.~

Gracie was ready to step up on the bus. "Whoa, ladies. No dogs allowed on the bus. Sorry."

Marge pushed herself in the doors. "This here is a helper dog. Can't ya see my friend is half-blind? They's always together."

The driver looked at the dog and wrinkled his nose. Gracie held the leash was wearing sunglasses, a straw hat, and had dark stains all over her hands and lower arms. "Haven't I seen you two, before?"

"Don't think so. But we need to git home. We road another bus here this morning with no problem. She's a good dog, no biting."

"C'mon." He nodded his head for them to board.

They took the back seat, and Sweetie curled up at their feet, content to be wherever they were. "Do ya mind if we change her name? I'd like Sweetpea better."

"Aw, that's a nice name. Wait till Valleen sees her. Boy, she'll be surprised."

Gracie proceeded to place her dentures back in her mouth. "Good idea you had there, that me with no teeth would make me look more pitiful."

"I get lots of ideas. I just forget most of em."

They laughed. Gracie reached down and scratched Sweetpea's scruff.

~.~

Valleen was stunned to see Sweetpea and the girls in such a state, paint and all.

The girls were shocked to hear that someone was looking for them. "That Ms. Harbo. She done got her thinkin all messed up. We paid ahead of time, didn't we Gracie? That witch owes us money. I think we oughta sue her for our money back. Whatcha think, Gracie?"

"I think, maybe we could put some wheels on this trailer and get out of town. I ain't goin back there."

"Are ya ponderin?"

Gracie slumped in a chair. "What if that old hag keeps lookin for us. Then what?"

"Listen to me. That guy talked to purt near everyone in the park, and far as he's concerned either they never heard of ya, or barely knew ya. I think you're in the clear."

She hugged each of them to offer comfort. "I'm not letting anything happen to either of you. By the way. Where'd you get that mangy mutt?"

twenty one

But Sweetpea's sweetness came close to being jeopardized rather quickly. "What in tarnation is that racket?" Gracie slid out of bed, looking around for her fuzzy pink house-shoes, and shuffled barefoot to the bathroom, which was Sweetpea's current bedroom.

The clumsy, long-legged dog had knocked over the waste basket and was wrestling with what looked like a dead rabbit, but in actuality, was one of Gracie's pink house shoes.

"Good grief, dog. Yuck, ya got em all wet and slimy. Guess you think ya finally caught up with a rabbit, don't ya? You're gonna be going to school real soon, no matter how cute you are." Gracie removed any other destructible items, rubbed the dog's head and said, "Good night, girly."

Gracie retrieved her violin after breakfast the next day and nuzzled with their new family member for a few minutes. "I'll be back in a bit," she said to Marge. Gotta get over to the home to play for the lunch crowd. Ya gotta take her out soon, now. Her bladder must be as small as mine."

"Aw. Wish I could go."

"She's too nervous to be left alone. She needs time to adjust. I won't be gone long."

It was a beautiful day, as most were, and the nursing home was just a few blocks away. Gracie looked forward to playing her violin for the residents there. They and the staff seemed to enjoy her music. Often she went into the rooms, or strolled down the halls to play for those unable to get out of their beds.

Gracie strolled the halls before lunch, since she was early, playing her music softly. The magical notes of *Fleur Elise* took many of the patients to a happier time, and made them smile. It made Gracie smile, also.

She, too, went to beautiful places when she played the bow against the strings. Sometimes she thought of her earliest childhood memory, which would bring a bittersweet tear or two. She smiled when she remembered her Dad before he died. Her memories of her mother remained shrouded by a mist, so long ago. She couldn't recall a pet of any sort that actually belonged to her. She briefly thought of Sweetpea's eyes, so full of affection.

She walked into the dining room, mildly surprised at how full it was. The first person she saw was the young activity director, Lindsey. Always smiling. Gracie didn't know what to think when everyone started clapping. She looked at Lindsey.

"What's goin on?"

"The residents all want to thank you for being so kind and generous. We enjoy your music so much and want to be sure that you know that."

Gracie's cheeks flushed as she turned around to see Charlie at the piano. He often accompanied her on the piano when she played the violin, but today he had already started without her.

"This is for you Gracie. We love your music." One resident gave her a giant card signed by everyone that could, and another handed her a small bouquet of yellow roses. Then they started yelling from their seats.

"We love you…You're wonderful…Don't ever stop playing."

"My goodness. Ya'll makin me get all teary-eyed." More clapping came. "Well. Thanks a lot. This is one of the nicest things that ever did happen to me. Maybe, the nicest. Y'all are all so sweet. Now stop making me cry. I'm gonna play somethin special for ya'll."

"C'mon, Gracie," Charlie said as he winked at her. "Let's play something rowdy."

"Tell you what. This violin can get as rowdy as I want it to."

"How about a polka. That'll get them going."

twenty two

Gracie plays her music at the retirement home, as often as she can. Marge and Valleen continue practicing for Marge's singing debut there some day. Marge really looks forward to that.

They play cards with Ivy, Zelda and sometimes Wilma a couple days a week. And Gracie plays her violin on piers around, close by, at least once a week. Most days, though, they sleep as late as they want, float in the pool, eat when and what they want, and, occasionally, head to the beach.

They eat meals with Valleen and Fred a lot, but sometimes they prefer to eat at their place or by the pool with their neighbors. Life is simple, most of the time. There's a few more things on their personal to-do list. Seems like every now and again something new gets added just for the fun of it. Like Marge had said, "It gives us something to look forward to. And, by golly, if it's on the list, it's going to get done some day."

Most of the time, if anyone wants to find Gracie and Marge, they'll be walking Sweetpea down on the beach or visiting friends in the Breezy Palms Mobile Home Resort Park. Sweetpea went most everywhere that Gracie and Marge went.

She always had them up bright and early each morning, howling to go outside. Life changed after Sweetpea came to live with Gracie and Marge. They had a sense of purpose now. They were responsible for something other than each other, and they liked it.

Of course, Gracie plays her violin every chance she gets. She has grown particularly fond of playing on the piers in the early morning hours. Valleen told her she would be glad to drive her sometimes, but the spoiled woman doesn't know what the sun rising even looks like. But the sunrise often beckoned to Gracie.

~.~

One magnificent morning after a light storm the night before, the sky shown indigo blue as it awaited sunrise. Gracie sat quietly on a wooden bench at about the half-way mark of the wooden pier. The pungent smell of fish, still clinging to the wooden tables where they had sucked in their last gasps of life the night before, still hung in the air. Silver specks from the fish scales dotted the tables and the deck underneath. All was quiet. Soon fishermen and vacationers would converge onto the pier, soaking up the morning sun and all the ocean had to offer.

She focused on breathing to the rhythm of the gentle waves slapping against the posts below, and smiled at the occasional rogue wave that sprayed droplets further up the tall timbers. Her eyes closed, body poised, and her hands rested softly, barely touching the violin resting on her lap. She waited.

She had awakened early, long before the sun would drench her home with the light of a fresh, new morning. Her sleeplessness reminded her of her treks to downtown Louisville on a quiet bus ride in those early morning hours, and long before that to downtown Indianapolis and St. Louis. Each time for the same reason, to play her lilting music in the midst of the hustle and bustle of other peoples' rushed lives. There, she escaped into the powerful calm of her own sweet noise until she no longer heard the cars, buses, horns and loud voices around her.

And so, here she was in a new city, a different kind of life, hustle and bustle replaced with an easy meandering by tourists and residents alike. It was easier to breathe here, more than anywhere she had ever been.

When it was time, she opened her eyes briefly and welcomed the first light of day as soft streaks of color peaked over the horizon. She whispered a quiet prayer of thankfulness. By the time the warmth of the sun's rays made their way to Gracie, softly washing over the pier in a bath of soft pinks and yellows, the well-worn bow and string had already claimed their stage.

Her soft music floated across the heavy boards, welcoming the day, the birds, the fishermen and, eventually, sleepy vacationers hoping to catch sight of sea turtles and *dolphins. The people were not disappointed if they hoped for an unusual experience to talk about later at the beach or over dinner.*

All morning, Gracie played her violin as families with eager little children came and went, couples, both young and old, strolled by holding hands. They smiled pleasantly. Some stopped while others slowed their pace. All heard the gentle beauty of the bow caressing the strings, and wondered a little at the sight of this amazing musician with her eyes closed and still in her pajamas.

Gracie knew they were there, that some stayed a while and took pictures, while others moved on slowly. Dollar bills dropped quietly into her violin case as she played. Some whispered so as not to interrupt the magic, thanking Gracie or bidding her a good day. She would nod in recognition or appreciation.

She silently marveled at how different it was, playing on a pier, at the edge of the ocean, from playing on city streets where people were embarrassed to acknowledge an old woman playing a violin who perhaps expected money. She did like the money, but she played because the making of music has always been her first love.

She would tell Marge later that the major difference is that she is now a revered, solitary artist sharing her gift of music, rather than someone to pity and feel guilty about.

Gracie liked it here. She liked the salty air. She liked the people drawn to the water in the early hours of the morning.

And then, on her own time-clock, Gracie opened her eyes, smiled at the folks standing around, packed her violin into the case without touching the money, and slowly, walked the length of the long pier. She stopped for a small bottle of orange juice and headed home, humming something from a memory of another time and another beach.

www.ingramcontent.com/pod-product-compliance
Lightning Source LLC
Chambersburg PA
CBHW071601200626
46811CB00027BA/862